FIRE MOUNTAIN

Continuing the story of the Shining Stone
BRENDAN QUAYLE

PART 2 OF THE TALES OF THE Q'ALIX SERIES

SilverWood

Published in 2025 by SilverWood Books

SilverWood Books Ltd
14 Small Street, Bristol, BS1 1DE, United Kingdom
www.silverwoodbooks.co.uk

Text copyright © Brendan Quayle 2025
Map illustration by John Booth
Copyeditor Emma Mulholland

ISBN 978-1-80042-297-1 (paperback)

British Library Cataloguing in Publication Data
A CIP catalogue record for this book is
available from the British Library

Page design and typesetting by SilverWood Books

DR BRENDAN QUAYLE is an award-winning environmental writer and film maker. He is the author (with David Bellamy) of the best-selling *England's Last Wilderness* and the seminal, now prophetic, environmental primer *Turning the Tide*.

Scots Irish of Manx ancestry, he lives with his family at the edge of a wild wood in the North of England.

Trained originally as an anthropologist, he studied amongst shamans and real-life sorcerers in the mountain tribes of the High Himalaya. His extraordinary experiences there, together with his lifelong interest in the myth and folklore of his Celtic ancestors, provide the inspiration and much of the source material for *The Shining Stone*.

Find out more at www.brendanquayle.com.

ALSO BY BRENDAN QUAYLE

The Shining Stone
Part 1 of the Tales of the Q'Alix series

For Lexi

PRINCIPLE CHARACTERS AND THEIR TRIBES

Osian, Albin Otar*; a hunter.

Caryn, (f) Eronn/Albin Otar; Osian's daughter.

Drion, Eronn Otar; Caryn's guardian.

Tiroc Og, Catton – Wildcat; shaman, warrior band chief.

Bran, Brach – Bear; warrior.

Gimin, (f) Ruadh/Rideag – Red Fox/Red Wolf; hunter-warrior.

Reyn, Ruadh – Red Fox; son of their chief.

Romi, (f) Tarsin, Flying Fox; an old pirate.

Lakon, Eronn Otar; Tiroc Og's first lieutenant.

Ganoc, Catton – Wildcat; Tiroc Og's second lieutenant.

Log Marten, Pinec; name unknown.

Cana-Din, She-Eronn Otar; priestess-warrior.

Gwion-din, Eronn Otar; an elder, her father; a ferry keeper.

Yamis, Barod – Beaver; warrior, boat builder.

Bron, Brach – Bear; Bran's twin brother.

Aridh, Aguan; Sea Gypsy, mercenary.

Garidh, Aguan; mercenary.

Iona, She-Eronn Otar; warrior.

Pone, Rhuad – Red Fox; warrior.

Ranig, Sideag – Grey Wolf; elder warrior.

Aehmir, Lepoch – Wind Hare; seer.

*Otar are a group of tribes whose totem is an otter, but of different types (e.g Albin Otar – Lake Otter; Eronn Otar – River Otter etc.

The Morok

Morok are a force of outlanders of unknown tribal origin under the control of the Ferok – Polecat tribe led by Kahl, a skryer and prophet, and Krachter, a Ferok, Kahl's lieutenant. They are allied to the Skraeling tribe whose totem is a shark and whose king is Iskar.

Note on Totems

The tribes distinguish themselves from one another through totems deriving from mythological ancestor animals, e.g, the Ruadh totem is a red fox, the Rigead totem is a red wolf, the Lepoch totem is a hare and so on. Totemic animals can be seen on warrior sword hilts and staffs, in their cloaks and head-dresses, and in body paint). In some cases, members of tribes display the physical characteristics, talents, abilities or attributes of their animal totems, e.g: Albin Otar (otter) are slim and are great swimmers and fishers; Catton (wildcat) have nightsight and curved fingers like claws; Brach (bear) are huge and thick framed; Sideag and Rigead / Rhuad (wolf and fox) are slender and swift-footed; and so on.

CARYN

aryn and I, her guardian, spent the day following the first part of my reading from her father Osian's journal largely doing winter tasks. I went down to the waterside to bring back more of the logs, pummelling my way through thigh high snow drifts, the air again so cold I could hardly feel my legs. We had planned to go to Yamis's place, spend the day in warm Barod company, and bring back some eggs, goat's cheese and honey for the larder, but the frequent snowfall and the height of the drifting meant we just had to make do at home and hope for better conditions tomorrow.

Caryn had been quieter than usual, mostly reading and doing clothing repairs and washing. She also offered to make the evening meal: 'Anything but fishmeal porridge,' she had said with a laugh, as she rolled up pastry for her best dish: a pie bake using up the last of the goat's cheese and some leek and turnip I'd retrieved from the snow that morning. I'd seen her glance from time to time at the jar above the fireplace, but she said nothing and asked no questions about what she'd heard the night before.

Then later, dinner over, we retired to the fireside and I re-opened the journal to the page where I'd stopped the night before. I expected I'd finish reading it before bedtime. The second, shorter, but even more extraordinary part of Osian's chronicle would have to wait for another night. She sat patiently waiting for me to begin, from time to time running a brush through her wonderful tricolour mane. And I began again, in the old way of all the tale tellers, though what she was about to hear, incredible though so much of it is, was no tale.

If all were told…

1

THE LAVA WOODS

We broke our fast just before daybreak atop a huge flat boulder overlooking the thick forests that lay around us. Far behind was a faint red glow – all that was left of Trisuldur, the enemy fort our company of renegades had destroyed; flames from the inferno leaping high into the night sky. Ganoc, our chief scout, had set explosive firelogs around the fort after we left, and they'd clearly done their work. But if we'd seen the sky light up, so too would others. And, I'd been told, no matter how devious the trail the leader of our little band, the Wildcat Tiroc Og, was taking, vengeful Morok forces would follow – and find us.

But the foot soldiers of Kahl the Skryer weren't the only threat. For in the woods we'd heard an eerie sound dreaded by all the tribes, interrupting us in our tracks and sending shivers down my spine: the deep throated, bloodcurdling howling of Okwa echoing through the forest like a storm of tormented ghosts. These giant sabre-toothed timber wolves – the most fearsome predator in all the continent of Manau – marked the remains of their kills with a scent from their glands like long-rotten meat that would turn any stomach. Ganoc said he'd already smelt their presence and seen tracks – invisible to most others except Wildcat trackers like him and Tiroc Og – crossing the very trail we were on. The prints were fresh. Okwa were around somewhere, aware of our presence, watching our every move, biding their time before attack. Were they to do so, few of us – if any – would survive.

Tiroc Og had offered a fragile reassurance, brushing the danger off, but, I noticed, with a check in his throat. 'They'll have smelt blood, back there, in the air from Trisuldur,' he said. 'And they'll have gone in that direction to look. Anyways, Okwa don't usually attack by daylight, but as we go forward, we must be as attentive as the small deer.'

The other warriors in the brave company seem to accept this, nodding their heads, but as we'd moved forwards, I noticed glances into the trees and weapons being readied: bolts being clutched beside the bows, knives and swords to hand. As for myself, I wasn't so reassured. Since waking I'd been feeling a cold tremor from the mysterious object huddled in the *papose* at my back.

The *Solon*, the Shining Stone. It was warning me. Danger. And near. But the sensation passed. We heard no more howling and our immediate attention was on our stomachs. I was so hungry that my share in our makeshift cook's meagre distribution of dried meat and thin oatcakes barely saw the sides of my mouth. Some warriors grumbled about the portions, casting suspicious looks at our cook, Bron, a great fur-clad Brach – Bear tribe – still eating long after the rest of us had finished.

'Funny how the last share is always the biggest,' Bran, his huge gap-toothed brother, and my more or less now constant companion, grumbled in my ear. Bron, seated slightly apart on the edge of the rock, munching away happily with his full set of teeth, seemed oblivious to the complaints.

'Our destination is yonder,' Tiroc Og said aloud, pointing his shaman's staff towards a row of hills in the misty norther distance. 'And maybe also our destinies.'

No-one replied, except to press Bron for another share-out. Shaking his head, the young Brach said, 'It has to last till yeh catch something. Drink water, it'll fill the gap.' Then he laughed, his fur cloak, replete with marten and mink heads, quivering as his chest heaved.

Tiroc Og, smiling thinly, sat back down beside me, pipe in hands. He, Bran and I were positioned on the rock slightly apart from the others – now busy with morning routines. I took the opportunity to ask more about Rakhaus, our destination: the remote fortification of the Morok, where my mother and father were being held as slaves along with others of the once free tribes of the Erainn territories, surviving victims of the Morok invasion that followed the onset of the Long Winter. Most of Tiroc Og's band of renegades had friends and kin that had been taken there, for whatever wicked purpose we knew not.

One of those being held was the revered Gwion-Din, an elder of the noble Eronn, the Otar tribe of Erainn – hereditary keepers of the holy lands. Rescuing him, I'd learned, was a key objective for Tiroc Og, who I met when I first arrived in Erainn from the Albin lands to the south, home to my ancestors. Though Tiroc Og, like Ganoc, came from a small colony of Wildcat in Erainn, most of whom had now left – or been erased. My own kind were Otar tribe like the Eronn, but from distant Alba. We didn't have the signature tricolour manes, gifted, it is said, by Yahl the creator god, to mark out the guardian tribe of the Erainn river lands – the richest of all the territories in the ancient continent of Manau and a place of pilgrimage.

Tiroc Og answered my query by saying, 'Rakhaus is on an island on a lake deep atop mighty Kariyag, the Fire Mountain,' while he scratched the sharp edge of his staff on a patch of crumbled stone and sand on the rock at his feet.

'Yes, Bran told me that much,' I said, turning to glance at my companion, but the giant Brach had wandered off – no doubt to press his brother for another helping of food.

'Look, I'll draw it out; 'tis a complicated situation, so listen close, an yeh can always ask questions later,' Tiroc Og said, glancing around – seeming to take in who was nearby. 'Here is the lake, a flooded lava crater. The waters are so vast that if yeh stand on one side you can barely see the other. 'Deed 'tis more like a sea than a lake. Atop a rock on the highest point of the island stands an ancient ruin from the ancient days, afore, 'tis said, even the time of the Manu. Over this Eronn and Wind Hare monks built a castle after the fashion of Erintor, home of the Marcher Lords, and named it Elvintal. But it was abandoned many moons ago –followin' the demise of the Lords – sometime afore the Marsh Wars.

When the Morok came they turned it into headquarters for thon devil Krachter, Kahl's chief lieutenant in the Northerland. 'Tis a natural fortification, shielded by deadly marshlands to the west and cliffs to the north which go straight down into the deeps of the lake. On the easter edge of the island there's a jetty fer the landin' of goods and slaves with Aguan boats that sail to and from a port on the crater rim. That's where the Morok troop camp is found: the place lined with a double row of barbed palisades, the ditches between filled with spike traps. The souther edge of Rakhaus – facing us – slopes gently into the lake. But this area the Morok have ringed with booby traps and spike pits and the waters are watched over by battle boats.'

'What about the norther sides of the island?' I asked, pointing towards the top of his sand sketch.

'That's where the cliffs are. And jes like the norther slopes of Mount Kariyag itself, they are impassable, even to the best of the climber tribes,' he said, pushing a few small stones in a line to represent them. Then, pointing to the edge of the crater rim, he added, 'Beyond the rim the mountain drops down into the Broken Sea, which is frozen for half the year; part of Arctos, the ice desert territory of the Red Skraeling.'

'The robber tribes?'

'No, not the same as the little Skraeling that roams the tribal lands. As different as a horse is to an ant, red-maned and bony-faced, like skeletons. Them are tall, strong and aggressive like Okwa, though rarely seen outside Arctos or its islands. Iskar, their king, is allied to him of the Morok – Kahl.'

'So Arctos is part of Kahl's empire?'

'Well, no, not that. But it's key to them. The largest of Arctos's countless islands, where Iskar dwells, Skraelandia, is where *petican* comes from. It's vile stuff – dried arctic meat, mostly whale, flightless birds and sea tiger. 'Tis what Kahl feeds his hideous troops with. Brought onshore by Skraeling ships to Agua ports on the easter coast, it's then taken over to and up the mountain and over the crater rim by Aguan mule fer transferring to the island.'

As I studied his drawing, I thought of the tactics Tiroc Og had used when we destroyed the Trisuldur – and how we'd severed a Morok supply chain. But before I could ask if he was planning something similar, Ganoc approached, a harrier on his shoulder, and whispered something in his ear.

Our chief pondered this, looking annoyed, then spoke aloud in Ironese to the bird. 'She must be there somewhere. Keep looking.' The harrier stared back at him, not moving. Then, oddly, Tiroc Og appeared to correct himself, changing his command to a series of grunts. This time the bird responded, squawking back at him, causing Ganoc some amusement. The bird then shook its feathers, suddenly took off and was gone from sight. 'Clachoile – maybe she's already there, in the caves?' he said, scratching his chin as he followed the flight of the bird as it soared upwards.

Ganoc responded reassuringly. 'Yahl willing, chief. 'Tis our best hope,' he said, before wandering off to join another group. To me the whole dialogue between the two Wildcats and the harrier looked odd – as if the spoken words were for other ears. Why did Ganoc smile? And why did Tiroc Og first address the bird in Ironese, when I knew they had another language between them?

Bran, who'd been sitting with Lakon, Tiroc Og's second lieutenant, a tall tricolour-maned Eronn, came over to us. 'I was explaining to Osian about the Red Skraelings, *petican* and the supply chain,' Tiroc Og said to him, pointing at the edge of his sand drawing, and drawing a line beneath the Kariyag range. 'Below here, to the south, Osian, is Clachoile, home to Bran and Bron's fathers.'

'Brach territory?' I asked. 'The Brach really allow them to pass so close?'

'Amon, their chief, is wary of making new enemies, with Aguan and Red Skraeling territories being so close. So far, he has refused to challenge their Morok allies, and as yeh might know has been smoking the pipe of peace with all the tribes since the end of the Marsh wars.'

'Chief Amon is too old to be deciding such things,' Bran interrupted with a snarl. 'There's others among us who don't fear the Skraeling so much – would stamp like horses' hooves on them, send 'em back to the deeps o' the ice deserts where they comes from.'

'Old Amon has the wisdom of the long years,' said Tiroc Og. 'His hand 'ill be a cautious one. It'd be a brave step, taking on all three tribes at the same time. Yer father'll be staying any move he makes, if any – till the time's right.'

'Amon – Bran's father…?' My mouth dropped open. I knew of the great warrior chief from Grandfather's accounts of the Marsh Wars. So, Bran and Bron were his sons – heirs to the vastness of Clachoile! And Bran, the elder, would one day have been chief of the most powerful tribe in Manau – had he not taken the rebel road. He and Bron were currently outcasts! I stared at Tiroc Og, who guessed my astonishment and waggled his eyebrows as though to say, *that's not the half of it.*

'Yeh should 'ave seen yer face, young Albin,' said Bran with a guffaw. He patted my shoulder and wandered off again, shaking his head.

'So, Tiroc Og, if an army of the free tribes were to reach Kariyag, which way would they come?' I queried, trying to grasp the options ahead for all – never mind the complexities of the company I was keeping. I'd been given to understand that the one warrior who could lead such an army was the renegade she-warrior, Cana-Din. From a hideout deep in the dark forests of the Terai to the south-east, she and her band of outlaws had been terrorising Morok with surprise raids, setting fire to their camps and fortalices. She alone, I was told, could persuade the free tribes to overcome their traditional enmities and act as one against Kahl and his murderous force, as the child of Gwion-Din, the Eronn elder whom Tiroc Og had committed his band to rescue.

'They'd have to come from the wester lands,' he replied, again in a raised voice, scratching arrows around his sketch of Kariyag. 'Any force assembled there would come up through the Karst then take a norther trail around Erainn, through the Kariyag range, then down towards the wester side of the mountain. The slopes there are deeply wooded, and they wouldn't be seen by Morok spies and scouts. Once up top and over, they'd gather unseen on the wooded western rim of the lake fer the crossing.'

'Crossing? Where would they land? You said the wester end of the island was where the deadly marshes were – how would that work?'

'There are means,' he responded with a knowing twinkle. But the Kariyag hills were deadly in winter and the Karst was home to Skarag, Kahl's dragon spies. It all seemed a bit fanciful to me and many moons in the doing, particularly as it seemed Cana-Din was said to be currently in Clachoile, thousands of leagues away on the far side of the Manau peninsula. But Tiroc Og casually drew a line in the sand towards the centre of his sand sketch and again, raising his voice, said, 'I can see yer not convinced. 'Tis a long and a dangerous journey, but the thing is, 'tis exactly where the Morok would least expect an invasion to come from. And as long as the army moves by night, enemy scouts would see little o'er such a vast area.'

He rubbed a hand over his eyes, then stood and walked towards the highest point of the rock. As I watched him go, I noticed out of the corner of my eye the Aguan pair, Garidh and Aridh, moving away from behind the rock. They, alone of the warrior group, had been in close hearing range, out of sight on the far side of the boulder. Tiroc Og, ever wary, must have known this. I wasn't the only audience. But at the time, thought little of it.

'Time to move out,' Tiroc Og suddenly announced, jumping down from the rock.

And so, once again, we took the trail, Ganoc leading the way. Later, walking alongside Tiroc Og, I asked about the castle on the island.

'Elvintal,' he replied, 'was built as a place for mendicants and tribal priests to live in peace and prayer. There's a moated sky tower, the Tor of the Winds, tallest building in all Manau, where they used to hang their prayer flags – and two other towers, where they lived. But the monks abandoned it many moons ago when their numbers declined, the remainder preferring to move around the territories and along the pilgrim routes where there were alms to be had and shelter. Elvintal had great beauty. I hates to think what the Morok have done to it.'

'How long before we get there?'

'It'll take two days and nights of quick marching to reach the foothills, another two to ascend the souther flanks of Fire Mountain. We'll climb at nightfall and rest along the way.' He paused. ''T'is my hope Cana-Din would already be in a good position.'

Not in Clachoile then? 'What if she doesn't show?' I queried, the question 'where is she?' on the tip of my tongue, though I didn't utter it.

'Then, Osian, we do what we can,' he replied firmly, waving a hand in the air.

We walked on in sombre mood. Without support, I was sure his expedition was surely doomed. Surely, he would change tack – maybe bide time in neutral territory till he was assured of backup. However, my own determination remained constant. My kin, if alive still, were in Rakhaus. If the company had to abandon their mission, and if I had to go to that place alone to try and free them, I would, whatever the risk.

'Shouldn't we wait a little longer for the harriers to return?' I blurted.

'No. There are Morok behind, tracking us. We needst move on, save our energies for what lies ahead, not risk an encounter.'

Bran, who'd been up at the front of the line, suddenly reappeared. 'Chief. New Okwa tracks up ahead.'

Tiroc Og glanced towards the front of the line, then at the heavens. The weather on this day had been remarkably calm; the sky grey and cloudy. But the very stillness of this landscape, the absence of birdsong or sound of any kind, even wind in the trees, was unsettling. Okwa! A shiver ran through me.

Then Lakon joined us from behind, catching his breath and said, 'Chief, I heard mastiffs in the woods to the easter side. Morok are most likely going to come round, try to cut us off.'

'So fast?' asked Tiroc Og. 'We'll needst then change direction, keep ahead of them. Bran, go back to the front and tell Ganoc that Morok hunting parties are coming on fast from two sides. Best if we all group together and change direction,' he said, pointing to the darkest part of the wood. 'Okwa now are the least of our worries,' he added.

It was an incredible thing to say. I knew how Okwa could appear in a flash and eviscerate their prey in seconds, tearing them apart limb from limb. When Grandfather spotted Okwa tracks, even old ones, on hunting trips in the Albin mountains, we always headed straight for home. At least with Morok we could evade or stand our ground.

'I'll let Ganoc know,' Bran said, running off and quickly returning with the others. Once we were together, Tiroc Og simply said, 'We'll go west from here, circle round and then rejoin this trail further along. Walk two by two and watch out fer enemy movement. Ye'll smell 'em first.' Then he forged waist high through thick brush, staff in the air so we could see him.

No mention of the Okwa. Bran took position beside me.

The forest here was becoming darker, but the brush thinned out as tree branches towered low over us. There was little light here. The trees were jet black and the ground at our feet not scattered with pines, but with dark ashy stones and pebbles.

'What are those?' I asked Bran, brushing my fingers against a tree. It was stone, not wood.

'They's lava trees,' he replied, matter-of-fact.

A petrified forest. I remembered we had some stone trees in Alba, on higher ground, but not like this, or so thickly clustered.

We proceeded in watchful silence, all eyes on the trees and rocks. Then the forest became so dark we could hardly see. Suddenly, I felt a tell-tale warning vibration in my lower back: the *Solon*, the Shining Stone, was alerting me to imminent danger. If it were Okwa, in this poor light we'd never see them before they were on us. By avoiding the Morok, were we going headlong into a danger even more terrible?

But the vibration lessened and gradually ceased. As I walked, I wondered, once again, how this the mysterious sealed object tucked into the base of my *papose*, a thing without the quick of blood or breath, could not just sense a threat, but could even intervene – for me, or it – when danger threatened. And I was being changed by its very presence; by its uncanny power! My step felt lighter, my vision clearer, my hearing sharper and my mood calmer. I had become more of a fighter, a fully-fledged warrior, stronger, more resilient. Even my moves, my reactions, were faster. The speed with which I'd half-dodged a fatal strike in the woods was nothing short of uncanny. A crossbolt fired at close range had glanced off my goatskin *papose* as if it had been forged in my father's hardest iron plate. In the event it was Gimin, the She-Wolf-Fox that had eliminated the threat, killed my assailant, but not before the *Solon* had first intervened. When I no longer carried it, what would be my fate? Would these strange powers – those interventions – be lost? What if I couldn't rid myself of it – was bound to it, or it to me, forever and a day – until the very end?

I should be warier, more concerned. But with every fresh encounter with danger, I felt more excited, animated, ready for anything. My strange acquisition seemed to have empowered me, made me more confident. If it was acting solely in its own interest, using me, then so be it. I had my own mission, and, despite the terrible odds and uncertainties, I was determined to fulfil it. I just had to hope that the *Solon*'s path into its destiny, its *almadh*, was, for the time being anyway, also mine.

We were now approaching a narrow pass through the gloomy forest, twisted branches arching across the way like giant insects frozen in time. Tiroc Og had changed the order of the line, me with him to the front, Bran immediately behind, Lakon now in the middle of the company, ever-watchful Ganoc taking the rear. We came to a break in the trees. Suddenly the *Solon* began to quiver, vibrating with slow pulses at first, then more urgently. Danger!

'There's something ahead,' I blurted, grabbing Tiroc Og's arm.

'Yes, I see a red glow. Halt, everyone,' he urged. 'Arm yer bows, wait my signal,' he added, pulling an arrow from his quiver and putting it to his long bow. Crouching, we drew our bolts. I tried to keep my breath calm and shallow. Tiroc Og looked back and made a sign. Lakon, the company's best scout, crept past us and went forward, low to the ground.

We waited.

After a few moments, we saw Lakon in silhouette, openly standing, his bow lowered, his mouth covered. He signalled us on. We walked forward. Then came the stench, sickening, cloying, tearing at the back of throat, worse than anything I'd ever smelt – even the stink in the cavern where I'd first seen the *Solon*. My stomach lurched. Some of the others – hardened warriors – were already retching, bending over as they staggered forward. Before us lay a truly horrifying sight: broken bodies strewn everywhere; severed heads with twisted faces; gore spread across the ground; torn limbs dangling from the trees. In the midst of it all a campfire glowed dully, remnants of cooking and food scraps scattered around. The source of the red light.

'Okwa!' I coughed.

'Yahl save us,' said Bran, holding his nose. 'Morok, 'tis 'em.' He gestured at the mails torn from the bodies and the abandoned weapons. We were looking at the remains of an enemy troop and their hunting dogs. 'Another party – mus' have come from the north, from Rakhaus, even.' Bran added, kicking a severed leg. Hateful though the enemy were, I felt a glimmer of compassion for them. Okwa were cruel and killed for the sake of it, rejoicing in the slaughter and the suffering of their victims, torn to pieces, half-eaten while they lived. Yet we'd heard nothing – the devil wolves had been and gone without making a sound.

'Okwa doin' our work for us,' Bran said, but without a hint of satisfaction.

'Why did the Okwa not attack us instead of them?' I asked.

'I don't know. They don't distinguish 'tween tribes,' he replied, spitting on the ground. 'This lot could just as easily 'ave been us, or our friends. Or maybe they jes' like the taste o' Morok. Could be jes' chance.'

Was it chance? I felt the *Solon* purring gently through the skin of the *papose* as I averted my eyes from the scene. Had it something to do with this? Was it gloating – pleased about the dead Morok?

Bran nudged a Morok crossbow with his toe, then pushed it away with a grunt of disgust. It was covered in blood. This company, far bigger in number than us, had been attacked as they sat around their fire; their rude benders torn apart, their meagre possessions scattered on the ground. But there were no wolf wounds upon the dead. No gnawed corpses or bones. This was unlike the devil creatures.

'Look, the Okwa haven't feasted,' I said.

'Probably too disgusting to eat,' Bran said with a grimace, showing his broken teeth.

'The pack'll still be roaming near,' said Tiroc Og, poking at the edge of the fire. 'Watch yer backs – remember they'll come when you least expect.' But the *Solon* was quiescent. I knew they'd gone.

We left the scene quickly, moving forwards again in determined silence. But there was a hesitation in Tiroc Og's step. I saw anxiety in his glances at the sky. Still no sign of the harriers.

When darkness was almost fully in, we came upon the scent of water. But there was a heaviness to it, something I couldn't place. We entered a clearing with a mist hanging above a slow running stream that folded away into the shadows. But this wasn't mist like I'd seen before. This was red, even in the night – the colour of blood. We stopped at its edge, the water just visible a few paces beyond it. Nobody seemed to want to go further. Behind me, the warriors were murmuring.

'Where are we, Bran?' I asked in a choked whisper.

''Tis the Kryx,' said the Brach, gazing into it. 'They say its colour is thus 'cos it washes over the souls of the *Katha*.'

'What?'

'The undead – locked 'tween living and dying. Those never been given departure by their kin, or 'ave done great evil. They'll try to trap yeh, take yeh below, but cannot touch yeh – unless...'

'Unless?'

He grimaced. 'Yeh falls in!'

I took a step away.

'The Kryx rises from under the earth in the heart of Fire Mountains, then opens out fer a while, as yeh see here, then disappears into who knows where.'

As we stood nervously hovering on the banks, Tiroc Og suggested that we camped here for the night, and pointed to a nearby copse a little way back from the water. Any other Morok tracking us, he said, would see what the Okwa did to their brothers and probably flee. But the watch would be doubled.

While we were setting up our benders, Lakon remarked, 'Aridh. Where's Aridh?'

No-one replied. 'When was the last time anyone saw him?' he asked.

Ganoc spoke up. 'He was behind me jes' after we left the Morok camp but was trailing, fer some reason.'

'Where's the other un?' Bran asked. 'Garidh!' he shouted. No answer.

'When did anyone see the Aguan last?' said Tirog Og, not looking particularly concerned, almost as if their disappearance was expected.

'That would be mid-sun,' replied Ganoc.

As we stood there came the sound that we all dreaded most: the baying of wolves. Okwa! Still out there somewhere. And knew we were here.

'Should we go back, chief – look fer 'em?' enquired Bran, with little enthusiasm.

'Back where? How far back? It's impossible, it's out of our way – and we might never find them,' said Tiroc Og with a dismissive wave.

'The Aguan'll have to find their own way now, if yet they breathe. Goin' back puts our mission at risk – and all our lives.'

It seemed brutal. Aridh and Garidh were of the company, had fought alongside us, covered our backs. I'd disliked Aridh on sight. But a death in the maws of an Okwa? It was unthinkable. Tiroc Og's apparent lack of concern seemed out of character given the risks he and Bran had taken to keep me safe. Then, how little did I really know him?

That night we put up the benders in two tight circles around the fire with me sharing Bran's. Rations of dry fish were handed out before we settled down in our blankets. Tiroc Og and the Rhuad – Red Fox tribe – were to take the first watch. I witnessed Lakon offering to take a double watch in place of Tiroc Og. 'Only yeh knows the territory,' he said. But Tiroc Og merely shook his head, took up his bow, sat on a rock facing the deep woods and stared into the distance.

In the event the night passed peacefully and we heard no Okwa howling. I woke to the sound of axes busily cutting into damp wood, rose and went outside. A bone chilling mist was rolling across our camping place from the river, a grey fog, unlike the blood red of the night before. Bran, up before me, proffered a breakfast of dry rations in a wooden bowl and as I ate, I watched the Barod, warriors of the Beaver tribe, hacking with *aber-axes* at four large grey logs peppered with what looked like bubbles.

'They's pumice logs, in case yeh's wondering,' said Bran, resting his huge chin on his staff. 'Tis extraordinary stuff, hardened foam, spat out by the dragons o' Fire Mountain, long, long ago; carves like butter and floats like willow bowls. They'll wrap bender skins round them, tightly tied, to keeps the water from gettin' in. But y'know the best bit…'

Yamis, the biggest of the Barod, who was working nearby, held up a dugout in one hand at Bran's signal and waved it at me. 'They's light as a pigeon feather,' Bran said. Yamis nodded, a broad smile on his face. 'Fer carryin'.'

'Carry? But the river's just over there.'

'We're to takes 'em up the mountain, fer to cross Krater Lake,' he said.

Though brought up around lakes and boats and fisher folk I'd never seen anything quite like the crafts taking shape before my eyes: boats made from peppered stone – that would float! I'd wondered before how we were going to cross a river and later a mountain lake without canoes. Now I knew.

I looked around for Tiroc Og. He was nowhere in sight, but his bender was already down, neatly rolled and lying alongside his long pack. I rose, collected my things and helped Bran pack down his large shelter.

The dugouts were ready by midday. Around mid-afternoon, Tiroc Og appeared, had a short conversation with Ganoc and Lakon, went away, then returning a little later, stood in the middle of the camp and called, 'Circle.'

We crouched round, with some good-natured shoving and pushing to be nearest to the heat of the fire, as he began to speak.

'We'll cross the Kryx just before nightfall. Once on the other side we'll take turns to relieve Yamis by carrying the dugouts towards then up the mountain and we'll take a night break halfway up at a hidden place I know. Meantime, everyone help with the boats, ready yer weapons and be prepared to go when I gives the command.' He stood down and the warriors went about their business.

There was little for me to do that day but watch as the boats were finished, so I sat with Bran by the fire and offered to sharpen swords and knives for anyone who brought weapons over. Bron sat with us, preparing packets of dried food wrapped in skin pouches for the journey ahead. Conversations were muted – and short. The whole day, Tiroc Og went back and forth into the woods, occasionally having brief words with Lakon and Ganoc. When dusk fell, we were ready. It was time to cross the Kryx.

At the bankside, Bron handed out tiny plugs of wax while Tiroc Og instructed us to shove them in our ears. 'It's for the cryin'. Remember the *Katha* can draw you in, take yeh to your doom, Yahl save yeh. Don't listen to 'em.'

Bran shrugged as he packed wax into his ears, urging me to do likewise, which I did. I couldn't really see how something that was half-dead could hurt us just by crying, but I'd long learned on my journey that there was no 'normal' in these parts. Duly we clambered into the stone dugouts and with warriors standing at stern and prow, lifted our paddles and glided in parallel formation into the red mist.

The dugouts floated high in the water despite their heavy loads and moved swiftly through the sluggish river. Midstream, I saw a ripple in the water and leaned over the edge to look. There below the surface hovered a hollow-eyed face, its mouth gaping wide. Inside the mouth was a darkness – a nothingness. I jerked back in fright, nearly falling out of the far side of the dugout.

'Best don't look,' urged Bran and I saw others averting their eyes from the water, many with tears running down their cheeks.

The current was strong and our progress slowed until it felt that we were crawling across the river. My gaze kept drifting to the side of the boat, into the sea of tragic faces, but in the end, I screwed my eyes shut.

I was much relieved when we finally beached, disembarking onto a black pebble shore backed by clumps of boulders and pine forest, the ground rising steeply beyond. Tiroc Og and Ganoc ventured briefly into the trees, presumably to scout the way forward and on their return, we set off uphill bearing the dugouts in single file. Pone, one of the Rhuad, walked ahead carrying a solitary firebrand. The ground underfoot was soft – pine needles and mosses, with no snow or ice; the air warmer than any I'd experienced since the Isle of Avalor. Steam rose from the rocks between the trees, vents emitting hot air from somewhere deep in the molten heart of Fire Mountain.

The trees – real pines – were straggly and needleless and no barrier to progress. We began to ascend, sometimes on hands and knees, the going steeper and rockier with every step. Tiroc Og led again, with Pone carrying the torch. Bran stayed close behind me as we weaved between giant boulders and the trees.

After many *hora* we reached a cliff face beside a roaring waterfall. Tiroc Og called a halt and wandered around the space glancing upwards, then after a brief word with his lieutenants, strode over to where we were filling our flasks from the edge of the fall. 'Bran, Osian, I'm saying to yeh what I've asked Lakon and Ganoc to tell the others: that if we haven't heard from Cana-Din by the time we reach the top I'm going to attempt entering Rakhaus without her. If we get there, the odds of the company alone succeeding in our mission, with everyone coming out alive, are low. So, each warrior must decide now for themself if they wants to go on, or waits here till our return… if we return. If you wish to go no further, no shame will fall upon yeh.'

'What about yeh, Chief?' said Bran. 'What will yeh do if any of us go back?'

His answer was instant. 'I'm going on anyways. I will jes' pray to Yahl that Cana-Din will somehow join – with an army of some kind.'

'Ye'd really go on alone?'

'Yes.'

Bran scratched his chin with his huge hand. 'I don't see how thon's possible.'

'What d'yeh mean, brother?' asked Tiroc Og.

'How could yeh be alone if we're with yeh?' retorted the Brach with a kindly laugh. 'Our ears have hearts, Chief – and they are open. The brothers talked through this 'ventuality that night at Trisuldur – hence maybe our broken heads thon morning after. Yeh and yer whiskers are never going to Rakhaus alone! I doesn't know about

Osian here, but I can speak for the others. It's all or nothin'. Where yeh go we go, even if 'tis to our doom.'

A grin broke out on Tiroc Og's face. He thumped his staff to the ground. 'My faithful friends, yeh do me great honours,' he said, a catch in his voice.

In the pause that followed I murmured to Bran, 'There was never any question of me not going on to Rakhaus, come what may.'

'Nor us. Anyways,' he said, slapping me on my shoulder, 'why wouldst any of us pass up the chance to kill more Morok?'

Tiroc Og addressed us again, a hand outstretched towards the steep rock face alongside the fall we had to climb. 'The way uphill from here is treacherous. There'll be boulder falls and steep cliff faces. Sometimes we'll be in the open. Up high there are no trees. There may be Morok scouts and no doubt there'll be Skarag looking down from above. We also needs to watch out for rock panthers and though 'tis unlikely on the mountain, roaming Okwa.'

We shouldered our packs while Tiroc Og added his instructions for the ascent. Ganoc and his Wildcat cousin, Sanic Ag, as the best climbers with the keenest eyesight, were to lead unassisted. Once at the top they'd throw down ropes for us and the dugouts to be belayed up. The Brach, Bran and the other two were the strongest amongst us, so they'd be the first to follow the Wildcats up then take over the belaying the rest of the company and the boats.

The rock face was deeply pitted with lava bubbles, providing holds aplenty for the scramble upwards with the ropes. A single firebrand had been lodged low in a crevice on the cliff face to light the initial ascent. Then we'd have to entrust ourselves to the expertise of the Wildcats and the strength of the Brach.

Ganoc and Sanic Ag reached the top quickly. The ropes came flying down. We then watched the Brach ascend – being hauled up in stages – and waited our turn. Looking around at my companions, I saw no fear in their faces. My tribe were swimmers and I'd never really climbed anything until my earlier experience up a tree with Romi, her tribe the Tarsin – Flying Fox – famed for their skills at heights and much sought after as sailors. For them, ascending high rigged sailing vessels in storms was second nature. That encounter, as I first entered Erainn from the Karst, was scary enough. At least this time, when going up, I wouldn't be able to see the cliff base in the dark.

I found myself looking around for Gimin, the beautiful flame-haired Rhuad-Rigead, half-Red Fox, half-Red Wolf, who I'd seen only odd glimpses of during the march from the skirmish at Trisuldur. As she'd made no effort to speak to me since then, I felt unable, almost embarrassed, to approach her. She was at the back of the group, talking to the Rhuad Pone, the light from the firebrand gleaming in her eyes. She caught my eye and I glimpsed a smile. I'd looked away to hide my blushes and when I glanced again, she was laughing with Pone. At first, I felt a pleasant shiver, imagining it was me she was laughing with. Then came something else, a new sensation altogether: a flash of envy. I was jealous! I felt ashamed and turned away.

Soon it was my turn to go up. A rope round my middle, I was hoisted into the air, being pulled up so swiftly that I hardly needed to climb, though my knees banged against the rock. Thinking of Gimin while I ascended seemed to somehow calm my fears and soon I was at the top and amongst the others. She was brought up just after, but didn't say anything to me.

The first ascent seemed to take the largest part of the night as we all manoeuvred and gathered on a thin ledge, trying not to jostle. The dugouts, tied to lines, were hoisted up at the end. The sure-footed Wildcat, Fox and Wolf warriors and the Eronn and the Brach made light of it. But lake dwellers like the flat-footed Barod and I, the only Albin Otar, were like fish out of water. Even with the hoist we were using our bodies in ways unnatural to us.

The first grey light of day broke as we rested briefly on a second ledge, much bigger than the first. I noticed Bran nodding at Tiroc

Og, indicating with his eyes a bird-like shape high in the sky, just a tiny speck, but circling directly above us.

'Yes. I've seen it,' Tiroc Og murmured.

'What is it?' asked Bran.

'The wingspan is big. Could be eagle, high mountain raven, maybe. Can't really tell from here. But not Skarag, I don't think.'

Then it was gone. The *Solon* at my back had been quiescent throughout. No warnings. Maybe just too far away.

Tiroc Og addressed us again. 'Brothers, we make our last ascent a little further round the mountain, west of here. There are caves up in the rocks amidst a boulder field which is all that lies between us and the mountain rim overlooking Krater Lake. They will make good cover. We can light a fire there and take proper rest.'

We proceeded without incident and arrived before dawn at an area of gently sloping ground strewn with massive rocks, among which were two large caves formed from lava bubbles. Once inside the nearest cave we lit a fire and we warmed quickly in the thin dry air. Dried game and *tai* were passed around while Bron prepared a meal of fish and vegetable.

I noticed that Tiroc Og seemed content to sit back and watch the fire. Something, it seemed, had been resolved. But when he caught my gaze, I saw a glimmer of something like concern. Was it for me – or about something else? But nothing was said. The moment passed.

During the meal, Lakon allocated the watches. Bran and I were given the last one. We were to be roused two *hora* before departure. And so, using my *papose* as pillow, one strap firm on my shoulder, I lay back on the soft black sand of the cave floor, huddled into my blanket and gazed at the shadows on the cave ceiling.

But sleep did not come easily. Doubts gnawed away at me: how we were going to enter Rakhaus; what would happen if Cana-Din's force didn't show; how I'd ever achieve my mission in such unlikely circumstances. And there came to mind that odd business with the

Aguan, no longer in the company, and, it seemed, so casually left to a terrible fate in woods stalked by Morok hunting parties, or worse – Okwa.

In the end I reasoned that the fates would deliver what they would. And, resigned to this, exhaustion took over and I drifted off.

2

BETRAYED

I woke struggling to breathe, a thundering headache pounding at my temples, a quaking at my lower back and a stinking rag clamped over my nose. I tried to lift my arms but couldn't. My hands had been tied together round a rock at my back. I pulled away but the movement burned the muscles in my shoulders. I was able to shake the rag away, coughing and hacking with disgust. Through half-dimmed eyes I saw a flurry of movement and heard a gruff voice say, 'I'm takin' it,' as someone reached behind me and tried to grab hold of the *papose*. The *Solon* quivered violently. 'No. Leave 'is pack,' barked another voice. 'Our instructions were to takes both together – it and 'im.'

Both accents were familiar. The first was Aguan, but the second I knew who it was straightaway, female but gruff, unmistakeable! Another stinking rag was slapped over my face, this time held in place. My head drooped, my vision fading to black. I was dimly aware of being carried, the shapes of twisted trees moving past me and a strong scent of salt, of the sea. We were going up, then suddenly down.

I woke to find myself seated in an open rocky area; my feet bound. I looked for my weapons but they were nowhere to be seen. My *papose* was still at my back, shoulder strap intact. I could feel the curve of the *Solon*, though now it was still. Around me was rough scrub – dead bushes and grasses between clumps of boulders. It was daylight and although my head hurt, it was less painful than it had been. My hands were still tied together, but in front so that I could lift them to my face. A bandage on my neck smelling of seaweed was seeping warmth into the back of my head. It was refreshing and the headache was easing. A salve? My drinking horn had been filled and was at my feet. I was able to drink. I thanked Yahl for that, at any rate.

I tried to work back over what had happened. I'd been asleep in the cave but suddenly woke to find someone holding one of those stinking rags over my face. The *Solon* had been quivering wildly. But there'd been no intervention, no light or time shifts. It too was caught offguard. Did it sleep? Or was it something else? I'd seen a face. Garidh! I'd been betrayed. I bit back the curses that came to my mouth. Why, *why* had Tiroc Og trusted them? What had they done to the others?

I heard footpads and struggled angrily against my bonds. I felt dizziness return. My vision began to fade, then that voice again, not Garidh.

'Osian. 'Tis yer old shipmate. I've come fer yeh.'

Half opening my eyes, through a grey mist I recognised Romi's scarred face and red pigtails. I tried to speak but all that came out was a groggy grunt. The She-Tarsin, of all creatures, here?

My head swam. My eyes wouldn't open properly. My bones ached. I heard Romi exchange a few words with another in hushed tones, in the language of the sea tribes. Though the words were unfamiliar, I could understand what they were saying: not as sounds through my ears, but as meanings that seemed to patter into my thoughts like raindrops, with a vibrating echo that made each meaning sparkle and glimmer. The *Solon* was somehow transfiguring the sounds they made into my head.

Romi was with Garidh, on the far side of a lava boulder, out of normal earshot. But I could hear and I lay listening, rage boiling inside. Romi, in league with a treacherous Aguan mercenary. Hard to believe, even harder for me to accept.

'Why can't we jes kill him and takes it?' Garidh was saying.

Romi, her voice shaking, snapped back. 'No, yeh can't do that.'

'Well then, we don't have to kill 'im,' replied Garidh. 'We could jes leave 'im heres to fend fer hisself. We can be in Rakhaus with thon thing in his *papose* by nightfall. Krachter, yer tellin' me, will reward us well.'

'Yeh can't just take it, Garidh,' said Romi. ''Member what thon other Ferok said – that which he carries inside is lethal. Look what happened to them Krol that wuz carryin' it.'

'That's jes' superstition. They drowned in a storm.'

''T'wasn't like any storm I'd ever seen.'

'Then why isn't the Albin already dead?'

'I dizzent know. It's jes' what I wuz told.'

'Ach. I'm still fer takin' it – leavin' the water dog 'ere,' Garidh said angrily.

I heard the tang of a sword leaving its sheath. 'Don't even think of it, yeh pirate,' growled Romi. 'Alive, he's our only ways to gets our rewards. I was told to bring 'im with it. And without 'im they might jes kill us. They's Morok, after all.' Romi's voice was troubled – she was unhappy about what she was doing. Then I remembered: she had a twin in Rakhaus. Romi was no friend to Morok. Was her "reward" her twin's freedom? Me for him? Even if so, it was still betrayal. I was no less angry and I was hurting.

'Anyways. Time's gettin' on,' Romi continued. 'We needs the norther winds o' the afternoon, 'member. He'll rouse properly soon. Go down to the water and mak' ready the sails. We must go in the *hora*, afore his friends wake and give chase. Now. Do it! Afore I cutlass yeh!' A sword was re-sheathed.

'Still thinks we should have killed 'em while they slept,' Garidh grumbled, 'so's they couldn't follow. You wuz wrong there, tree-dog.'

'No, Garidh. That's downright murder as befittin' only the lowest o' buccaneers,' Romi snarled back. 'And yeh'd never've managed to kill 'em all afore they started comin' out o' the marsh gas. Anyways, yeh pirate,' she added in disgust, 'yeh were un of 'em, fought with 'em, lived with 'em. 'Ese were yer brothers in arms, yer friends. Why d'yeh wants to kill 'em?'

'I wuz never un o' them. Being with them 'jes suited me. I got moonsilvers. And the Morok knows they are coming – will kill 'em all anyways.'

I shuddered. Had Tiroc Og been leading us unwittingly into a trap? I knew our chances were small, but if the Morok knew we were coming we were surely doomed.

'I never agreed to any of that, Garidh,' said Romi, her voice shaking with anger. 'I am doin' what I have to – fer my own kin. After Kami is freed, I hope Kahl and his ilk rots to nuthin'. If thon Cana-Din, the Brach, an' their friends can defeats 'em in the end, then so be it – it be Yahl's will. If we gets the chance, Kami and I would join 'em. N' free this one too. I'd relish puttin' thon half blind Ferok, Krachter, to th' plank I tell yeh. First, we have to do this. I have no choice, n' may the gods forgive me.'

The Aguan snorted. 'So, what next, then?' he said. 'Yeh're supposed to be the clever one – or so yeh say. So how d'yeh make sure the Morok gives us what we wants?'

'Leave it with me. I've a plan for the Albin. Yeh be on yer way – get that *scud* ship-shape and ready to sail as soon as thon wind gets up.'

Garidh grunted and walked away. Then I heard Romi's steps, coming towards me. I'd little choice but to play along, suppress my fury, find out whatever I could before deciding what to do. Don't let on I knew what they were up to. One thing, my friends were alive; only sent to sleep. But when they woke would they come for me?

I pretended to snore. She came up close, untied all my bonds, put a hand on my shoulder and said, 'Wake up, shipmate. Yeh've slept long enough. Time to be goin.'

I half-opened my eyes and stirred. 'What? Where am I? Who's that?'

'It's me, Romi. The Tarsin. Remember the treehouse?'

'Romi, is it really you?' I spoke.

'Yeh must come with me, quickly now.'

'Come with you? Where are we going?'

'We're goin' to Rakhaus, Osian. There's a boat: a proper sailin' scud. We're goin' to save yer kin and also mine. I'll explain as we go. ''Ere, I'll 'elp yeh up.'

'What of the others, those I was with?' I said, pretending to let her help me up, but rage tightening the muscles in my arms and balling my hands into fists. 'Where are they? I hope you haven't harmed them.'

'We surprised the watch, gagged and tied 'em. We sent 'em all to sleep in their hammocks wi' harmless reed gas while we tooks yer.'

'Are they alright?' I snapped.

'Don't worry about 'em,' she replied. 'They're where we left 'em, all unharmed – but yeh wuz as safe with 'em as a fish among the sharkies. Their mission is sure to end in their death. And one thing yeh should know: theys not what they seem. They wuz usin' yeh – an' thon thing yeh carry. Yeh wasn't safe. That's why I had to take you.'

'Why do you say it's sure to end in death, Romi?' I tried to ask in a matter-of-fact way, shakily getting to my feet, stretching my arms and yawning.

'The Morok knows they're coming – expecting 'em – have been watching 'em all along, have set a trap for 'em soon as they land. They knew they'd try to rescue Gwion-Din; they're using him as bait. If you go with 'em, you'll be killed alongside the rebels. But Krachter has assured me of yer safety – if I bring yer to him. He promises the release o' yer kin.'

I sank to the ground, weary and forlorn, momentarily unsure of what – who – to believe. I'd assumed she'd been working with the rebels and now it turned out she'd been making her own plans all along. She was someone with whom I had a life-debt. We'd shared our stories. And now she'd become my enemy, happy to watch Tiroc Og's company walk into a trap – betray them. How could I trust her? Had she saved my life – took me up a tree to get away from Krachter – to use me as a bargaining tool? This couldn't end well. She said herself the Morok couldn't be trusted. It just didn't make sense. What was I going to do? If only I could clear my head, find a way of turning the tables. Involuntarily, I groaned.

''Tis jes the gas makes yeh weak. 'Tis harmless,' she said. 'Will soon wear off.'

I dragged myself to my feet. 'Why should I trust your word, or the word of this Kahl, if he says I and my kin will be safe?'

'Yeh've no choice, Osian. I've saved yeh – and yer friends – from certain death on Rakhaus.'

'How do you mean, you've saved my friends? You've left them to walk into a trap!'

'Nay, I told the Barod guards about the trap as I trussed them up. I urged them to tell Tiroc Og they should return to Erainn while they could.'

Could I really believe this? Besides, I thought, Tiroc Og was cunning enough to know if a trap was being laid. Even if he wasn't, I couldn't imagine him being turned back by advice that had been given by someone who'd just attacked his troop. Romi's dubious bargain with the Morok would surely end up killing us all.

'Ah, young Albin, what choice do we have?' She continued. 'The game is up. Yer renegades are vastly outnumbered. The Brach and the

Sideag won't anyways rise for an Eronn – even the glorious Cana-Din. Give 'em what they want, I say, and pray to Yahl they free our kin and let us go.'

I had to play along, somehow foil Romi's plan, find a way of getting back to my friends and warn them of the trap. I thought about the *Solon*, how it had kept me alive thus far. Whatever was guiding it, I had to hope it would continue to help me. As it was, I was weaponless and a poor match for my captors.

Romi shuffled her feet, toying with rope ends, her face anxious. I thought about my first encounter with her: the comical amble, the jokey demeanour, the clumsiness. I barely recognised the fearful creature in front of me now. Even her sea-speak seemed to have half disappeared. Which was the act – Romi the friendly old seadog or Romi, coward, traitor and Morok ally?

'You've made a pact of some kind with the Morok, which may or may not be worth a candle,' I eventually said. 'But you yourself warned me against them – even helped me escape them. Why would you believe them now? Once I'm in their power, would they really let me and my kin go free?'

'Them Morok devils could'ne be knocked off their decks by an army of buccaneers, never mind a handful of land-lubbin' renegades. They're cut-throats, only interested in treasure; the only ways to better 'em I reckon is to trade with 'em, desperate though it may seem to yeh.'

'Romi, I doubt that. I mean to rescue my kin, whatever the cost to me. But I won't double cross my friends.'

'There's no question of that,' she said, oddly satisfied with this response. 'Like I say, I've warned them already. Now we go to Rakhaus.'

'Where are my weapons? I want them back.'

'I can't give 'em to yeh till we reach Rakhaus. They're already on the *scud* – with Garidh. The winds are up. We needs move quickly. This way. Yeh first.'

I nodded, affecting a troubled acceptance of this as we slowly wound our way down through a series of clumps of jet-black pockmarked boulders until a huge vista opened before us: a pebble shore at the edge of a vast sweep of dark lake that stretched to the far horizon, empty except for a single mound that from this distance looked like a pointed anthill. We were over the rim of Kariyag. This was Krater Lake and that island must be Rakhaus!

At home it would take days of sailing to get to a place that distant, for lake winds tended to go in all directions and there were often sudden calms. But I was an experienced lake sailor. I knew how to use the weather to my advantage – to try an escape. And although I had no weapons, I could now move freely.

I glanced behind to see where we'd come from. The crater rim was behind us, a black wall that reared up from the beach. If Romi was telling the truth and it was only reed gas, my friends would be awake by now on the other side of it and deciding their next moves. I'd little doubt Tiroc Og could find Romi's trail and track us to here. But would they follow? It would be madness, surely. For their sakes I hoped they wouldn't. I was on my own now. The Wildcat, if he was to continue his mission, surely would just abandon me to the fates.

We began scrambling between clusters of smaller bubble-shaped boulders and large pebbles that shifted and quivered around our feet. Romi kept glancing behind, making me worry for my friends' safety – if indeed they were following.

We neared the water. In the shallows floated the sail craft Romi had mentioned, a small Aguan *scud*, such as I'd once had seen sketched by a visiting Aguan trader. These were a tiny version of the huge ships with which they roamed the high seas. This one had three sails and a high prow bearing the Aguan totem of a sea monster, mouth open, teeth bared, angry-eyed. Dark purple sails flapped uselessly in a wind that wouldn't take a sailboat anywhere. Garidh was there, standing on shore holding the boat with a rope, impatient, lip curled, posture threatening. I felt my stomach churn, anger rising to my throat, and as we neared I felt an urgent quivering at my back. The *Solon* was warning me.

Not for the first time on my long journey, I felt like a leaf being blown by the wind on a tree that one day would crash to the ground, toppled by forces beyond me – including the strange object in my *papose*. But I wouldn't turn my back on those who'd helped me.

Somehow, I had to escape, put aside my own mission, find my friends and save them from the trap they were walking into. Were I to somehow succeed in rescuing my kin, it would be without meaning if it involved sacrificing the lives of Tiroc Og, Bran and the others. And then there was Gimin. As I thought of her, I felt a lump in my throat and a stir in my chest.

I was reminded of lines that Grandfather had often quoted to me, said to be the words of a great warrior from the far-off days of the Manu, who'd set them down as he prepared to do battle against his enemy: "*He either fears his fate too much or his deserts are small, that puts it not unto the touch to win or lose it all.*"

The pebbles grew smaller as we approached the water. The shifting ground caused Romi, unsteady on her bandy sea legs, to trip and fall, ropes flying in every direction. This was my moment to turn and run, but Garidh had his crossbow already armed – a barbed bolt aimed straight at me. 'Don't even think of it, water dog!' he yelled. 'Run and ye'll be kissin' 'em stones with this bolt in yer heart.'

Instead, I bent and helped Romi to her feet. As I leaned over, I noticed an angular white stone among the dark round pebbles. As I lifted her up, I was able to pull the stone upwards with my feet and angle it towards the water. An upright. A god stone. A marker for me to show me the way back – and my friends to know where I was.

Suddenly Garidh started walking towards us up the beach, crossbow raised ready to fire. I felt the malice of the Aguan entering my skin as if it was the cold steel of his blade, the lethal curved spike of the sea tribes. As he came close, I could smell his breath. Rotten, like his teeth: a traitor's breath. He barked something at Romi. The old She-Tarsin, immediately upright, snapped back, ropes swinging at her midriff, her words incoherent, yet through the rhythmic quivering of the *Solon* their meaning seemed to drop into my head.

'The *scud*'s ready, but not the winds, tree dog,' grunted Garidh.

Hand on her cutlass, Romi said, 'We get on the water, Aguan, and wait. The winds'll come. They'd better.'

'Else?'

'Else, back there I heard the Wildcat's conch.'

'What! Told yeh we should've killed 'em,' the Aguan screamed at her, a flicker of fear crossing his face.

'Naught we can do about that now. We'll get on board, push out and wait.'

'Why 'ave yeh untied the the water dog?' Garidh responded, eyes darting glances between me and the crater rim.

I followed his glance and turned, my heart racing – a conch call! Maybe when I was still out of it? I gladdened; Tiroc Og was coming. The nearest boulder cluster was close. But could I reach it without a bolt in my back? It didn't look good. And my legs were still shaky. I hovered on the brink of running, but hesitated. Garidh must have seen it, for his blade was at my neck, the point digging into my skin.

'Into the boat, water dog,' he snarled. 'Don't even think of runnin'.'

'There's no need for that,' barked Romi, pushing away the Aguan's weapon with the point of her cutlass. 'He has to be alive, remember?' She turned to me before saying in Ironese, 'Goin' forward is our only hope. He'll kill us both without a thought.'

44

Garidh grunted and strode towards the boat, his blade flashing as he returned it to his waist-belt. Romi was all that stood between me and a knife in the back. Yet the *Solon* had fallen still.

Was this a signal? 'Go. Don't fight. Don't flee.' And if so, should I trust it?

3

KRATER LAKE

The lake shore shelved deep; the water a reddish-black, unwholesome colour, reminding me of the river Kryx – of the faces and the strange red mist that hung over it. These lake waters were its source. If it was as dangerous as the Kryx and I did manage to catch my captors off-guard, swimming for the shore wasn't an option.

The Aguan held the *scud* steady while Romi ushered me onboard and signalled for me to sit at the prow, just below the totem, while she took seat in the middle. Garidh then loosed the craft from the rock, jumped aboard and took the tiller. Almost immediately the winds came up. The mainsail flapped then filled and the little craft launched with slick ease into the dark red vastness.

'Will Krachter his-self meet us in Rakhaus?' Garidh shouted to Romi as he swung the tiller round so that we faced the island, the south-westerly wind at our backs now firing us speedily across the water. His words were blank to me, but their meaning dropped into my head, again with the slight vibration at my lower back. I noticed

Garidh's hand on the tiller was shaking and his eyes were darting suspiciously between me and Romi. I could see neither trusted the other.

'Kahl'll be there in person,' Romi shouted over the wind, taking hold of the mainsail stays and adjusting the boom to stop the boat tilting in the furious blast. 'They messed up before, when the Krol lost thon thing in the storm before hefted itself to the Albin – fer reasons beyond mortal ken. I wuz told they aren't to be separated. Krachter hissel' made me a firm bargain. "Deliver the Albin and his *papose* to us, Romi," said he, "and not only will yeh be free, but none will interfere with yer tribe again." So, he lives and we live. But I required Kahl to be at the exchange – jes' in case Krachter had his own designs on the thing. An' this wuz the agreement.'

The Aguan lapsed into a surly silence, occasionally fidgeting with the sword at his waist, his hold on the tiller erratic. At one point the boat sailed too close to the wind and lost power completely. The next second, the sail fully filled and the boat keeled sharply, almost pitching us into the water. Desperately wrangling with the ropes, Romi screamed at him. 'Get hold, Aguan, ye'll overturn us at that!'

I stared at the island, still a dot on the horizon, wondering what lay ahead: I was to encounter Krachter, maybe even Kahl the Skryer, the force behind the regime that had brought Erainn to its knees. Hopefully there, I'd discover why he wanted the *Solon* so badly – and me, it would seem. Foremost in my mind now was the worry about my friends. I looked down at the water: there were no *Katha* crying out, no undead visible beneath the surface. Should I just take the chance, swim for it while I could still see the shore? But I'd probably not make it. In these winds my captors could easily turn and outrun me.

The craft juddered erratically. Romi shouted to Garidh, 'I'm coming back to take the helm.' Adjusting the stays of the headsail, she pushed past me towards the stern and made to grab the tiller.

47

But to my astonishment, Garidh, with a violent move, shoved her away. Romi launched herself at him, knocking the tall Aguan on to the deck. The pair started to struggle. Simultaneously my eye caught a movement high in the heavens. A large bird was circling above us.

I looked down again at the dark waters and back at the shore, growing ever more distant. If I was going to jump, this was my moment. I scrambled to my feet, but suddenly felt an icy tremor up my back. The boat wheeled, lurched, and tumbled me back to the deck. Getting up I saw Garidh was at Romi's back and was pulling a rope tight around her neck. The tiller was loose and spun wildly. The mainsail flapped free and the boat wheeled again. Romi was on the deck making choking noises. Garidh used his foot to steady the tiller, pulled a stabbing knife from his waistband and aimed it at me. But suddenly, a blast of wind seized the mainsail, causing the *scud* to lurch. Garidh fell backwards against the mast, his weapon clattering to the deck. I dived to the back of the boat and grabbed the side to steady myself.

But Garidh was already on his feet and picking up the knife. Abandoning the tiller in his rage, he was coming at me. Suddenly, another gust of wind came up and caught the mainsail. Unchecked, the boom wheeled round and crashed with a sickening crunch into his face. It was enough to kill him, yet somehow, he managed to stagger to his feet. Jumping over Romi's inert form he came towards me again. But he faltered, horror in his eyes, blood pouring from his mouth. Then he seemed to just crumble, dropping backwards, hitting the side of the boat then tumbling towards the water.

The instant he broke the surface there arose an ear-shattering sound, a scream that was a thousand screams piled upon one another that gathered in pitch until it reached a crescendo, then suddenly stopped. In the eerie silence that followed I could hear nothing – not even my breath. It seemed like the world had stopped moving: the lake water still as glass; the *scud* suspended in a steep pitch half out of the water. Romi, lying on the deck, frozen like a corpse, me pinned to the side of the boat by some unseen force, unable to move. Garidh was half submerged in the water, a wave frozen mid-descent over him. Out of the silence there gathered a humming sound like the buzzing of far off insects. Then came a flash of green light. Everything shimmered like fresh leaves in the sun: the boat, the water, the sky.

Then, just as suddenly, real time returned. Everything rushed back in. The wind pounded the sails, creating fresh mayhem on board. The keel had dropped back in the water. We were swirling aimlessly, the boom swinging from side to side. I scrambled under it, clutching the bottom boards and managed to free the rope around Romi's neck, grab the tiller and the mainsail stay. The vessel immediately righted, the sails shaking free.

Romi groaned, holding her throat and gasping air. Pulling herself to her feet, she shot me a submissive glance. Holding on to the tiller, I threw her the mainsail stay. With one hand she hauled us steady then between us we managed to halt the craft's wild motions. I shouted, 'We're turning back,' half expecting her to resist; ready to force her if I had to. But before she reacted a hand appeared at her back over the side. Then a head. Garidh! His face was pulped and bloody, his cutlass in his teeth.

'Romi, watch out!' I screamed. But too late. He'd grabbed one of her pigtails and was pulling her head back. Her chest flew up, making her lose control of the stays, on the verge of tumbling over the side, when a geyser of foam flew out of the water and soared high above us with a roar like an exploding volcano. Out of the foam a giant scaly tentacle lashed the air and whipped itself around Garidh's neck. His eyes widened, his mouth dropped open and he was pulled back into the water. I saw him trying to claw at the tentacle with his nails, his face turning blue. Then, with a screaming, choking gurgle, he was dragged below. The waters stilled and a pool of blood floated to the surface.

Romi, half standing, grabbed hold of the stay. The boat steadied again. My heart was racing, my mouth full of bile. Garidh's blade was lying on the deck. I picked it up and shoved it into my belt. 'Go about!' I shouted, pulling the tiller to turn the craft into the wind. We were now facing shore, the sail straining against the relentless south-westerly. Then the winds eased and came around, gently nudging us back towards the rim. I looked back to where we'd been, half expecting the Aguan to surface. But of Garidh and the beast that had claimed him there was no sign. I felt no pity: he'd met his just deserts – a traitor's death.

I turned my attention to the other traitor. Her head hung, down her body was trembling. She looked up at me, catching my gaze. Her eyes were huge and dark with terror, darting between me and the *papose* at my feet where the *Solon* snuggled deep.

'We need to talk,' I said.

'Jes' keep thon evil thing away from me,' she blurted, pointing to the *papose*. She'd seen an intervention from an unknown force. For a superstitious seafarer that meant one thing. Sorcery! It was of *that* she was terrified.

Stunned though I was by what had just happened, part of me still couldn't believe that I – or rather the thing I carried – was capable of doing such things. Little wonder it inspired complete terror in others. 'It won't harm you,' I said in the end. 'Unless of course I let it,' I bluffed. 'I want an explanation, Romi. Tell the truth, or else...' I tilted my head towards my pack.

'I'll tells yeh everythin' I knows, onythin' yeh wants, young 'un,' she squealed.

'Well, how did you come to be in league with the Morok, and with Garidh? All that stuff you said up the tree. I thought you were a friend. And you were friends with Tiroc Og, too – one of the renegades – yet you betrayed them too.'

''Tis not what yeh thinks,' she said tearfully. 'I can explains.'

'No lies, Romi. Tell me how you came to deal with Krachter – the truth now, or you'll follow Garidh.'

She sobbed, loosening the stays. The boat began to drift as the wind came aft. 'Take care,' I said and she tightened her hold. The craft righted, closer to the wind, but still heading back to the shore.

'Jes after I saw yeh on 'em pines I got caught by 'em Morok pirates – careless, like. They'd heard me signalling – knew where I wuz. Were waitin'. When I dropped to the ground like a landlubber to collect kindling fer me fire they wuz all around me.' She paused to wipe tears from her face.

'Yes – and then?' I spoke. I pitied her suffering, but I would not show it.

'Well, the devils took me to thon Ferok we saw below thon tree – the one with the eye-patch, d'ye remember? It were Krachter hisself. He told me they had Kami – my twin – on a rack in Rakhaus awaitin' terrible torture. If I wanted to keep 'im from sufferin' I had to do their biddin'.'

The Ferok I'd seen when I first entered Erainn – the hawker with the eyepatch – that was Krachter! 'And you believed him, Romi, with all that you know of them?'

'What could I do, young Albin? I couldn't stand the idea of Kami in pain. Us Tarsin tribe, we are so few. If me and Kami die, we're in danger of being wiped out and earnin' the curses o' our ancestors.' She dropped her head again and sobbed.

I shuddered, struggling with the thought that Romi and Garidh were really going to deliver me up – a deal I was sure the Morok would have no intention of keeping.

'And Garidh?' I asked.

'Like all his kind, he's wuz in it jes'fer moonsilver. I'd been following yeh all by sailin' through the creeks, then when I found Garidh in the black woods – lookin' fer a Morok band, I realised he

51

wuz a spy all along, so I thought he'd be useful to me and suggested he come on board.'

'On board your treachery, you mean,' I snapped. 'What about Aridh? Was he a traitor too?'

She shrugged. 'I didn't see any other Aguan.'

We were tacking endlessly to stay on course but still too far from shore. And I was getting more nervous by the minute. We had to go faster. 'So, what exactly did you agree with the Morok, Romi?' I said, moving the tiller to right the drifting craft. Thankfully the sails filled again, but progress was too slow.

'Krachter said if I brought yeh and yer pack to Rakhaus they'd be waitin' on the shore with Kami. And we could use this here *scud* to leave. Kami and I wid be given safe passage once they haves what they wants.'

I could imagine how that would have played out: the volley of barbed bolts raining down on them as they cast off. It was naive to say the least.

She shakily pointed to the *papose*. 'Yeh just don't know what yeh have in there, how dangerous it is. Yer better off rid o' it.'

'Do *you* know?' I replied.

'All I knows 'tis an instrument of doom. And, young 'un, thon thing has changed yeh.'

'How so?'

''Tis in yer face, how different yeh are from afore. Yeh nows 'ave the look of a killer – like one of Tiroc Og's bandits.'

'Yes, I'll kill for my kin and my friends. If it means the death of those in my way then so be it.'

'That's as may be,' she spluttered. 'But that thing… It'll destroy everyone around it. Look at thon pirate Garidh, how he died; terrible, it was, even if… even if he deserved it. What's it to you – to us – if they devils have yer thing. Let 'em, I say!'

I gritted my teeth. I wouldn't let them have it. Somewhere inside me a small voice asked, *but why?* Why not give up the *Solon* if it meant saving my kin? What did it really matter to me, after all? I dismissed the idea straightaway. Once the Morok got what they wanted they'd certainly kill me – and my kin – were they even living still.

The wind changed again, the mainsail flapping. I went about and tacked and Romi instinctively shifted the boom. As we worked in stony silence, I heard a distant, throaty croak and looked up into the sky. From the direction of Rakhaus, two flying creatures came into view: huge, dark, skimming the water.

The *Solon* quivered violently.

'Skarag!' Romi screamed.

A squall rocked the boat.

'Quick, Romi. Tighten the mainsail!' I shouted. 'We can outrun them.'

''Old on tight!' she shouted back.

The *scud* lurched, its prow leaping out of the water with the force of the wind. The shore was closing but the Skarag were coming fast, one in front of the other.

'Look out,' she yelled.

Too late. With a great screech, one of the lizards plummeted towards us, talons extended. I threw the tiller to the side. The mast tilted. The boat swung round. The Skarag swished past, circled and came again. This time, straight for me. I tilted the boat again. The dragon missed but its flying claws sheared the mainsail at the masthead. A great tear ran down the cloth. The boat came to a shuddering halt and swung round, the wind clattering at the foresail.

The Skarag had circled and was heading back – straight for me.

Romi jumped up, landed between me and the oncoming lizard, raised her cutlass and cried, 'Tak' this, yeh flyin' frog!' and struck out. The creature swerved away, but not quickly enough. The blade caught its lower body, severing talons and slicing straight through the tail. With a bloodcurdling shriek, it toppled backwards into the water.

The boat was now spinning in furious circles, the winds pummelling the foresail. I left the tiller and dived across the boat to release the stays holding it taught.

'Look out! Behin' yeh!' screamed Romi. I turned and saw the other Skarag hurtling towards us. We both ducked just in time. I felt its talons graze the top of my head as it flew over. Then it swung round and attacked again. I ducked but it managed to sink its claws into my *papose* and before I could prevent it, it was being dragged high into the air.

I felt a lurching in my chest. It was as if my heart had leapt out of my body, taking all the warmth in my blood with it. Then from my throat came a sound that was not my own: an unearthly, ear-shattering scream. As had happened before, time slowed and then stopped. I saw the veined yellow eyes of the creature and its leathery wings, frozen in mid-air.

Then just as suddenly, real time returned. The Skarag reared up as if struck by lightning and dropped the *papose*. It clattered on to the deck and slid under an oar. Enraged, the creature turned and flying low, stretched its talons out towards me. This time I couldn't go lower, couldn't dodge the blow. Involuntarily I shut my eyes.

'No!' I heard Romi scream. When I opened my eyes, I saw that she'd leapt in front of me, cutlass raised, the Skarag's talons already sunk into her. The boat had become a maelstrom of talons, scales and teeth, flying ropes and flapping loose and torn sails, with Romi and the dragon locked together in a bloody embrace. I saw her raise her arm in a slow determined movement, saw the cutlass coming down and heard it cutting into flesh and bone. I ran at the Skarag with Garidh's blade. But the boat jilted, sending me backwards and tipping Romi and into the water, the creature's talons embedded in her chest. She writhed on top of the creature, her face twisted and her mouth gasping. I reached over the side to grab her, but she was too far away and was dragged under. Then, in a sudden rush of bubbles she surfaced, cutlass in the air, free of the lizard, a grim smile on her face. The foam around her was red with blood and flecked with scales.

'Grab this,' I shouted hoarsely, throwing the loose end of the jib rope towards her. But she didn't take it.

'Young un,' she gasped. 'I'm bad wounded. ''Tis my time. I'm goin' to the *sidhe*. Go back while yeh can. Find Tiroc Og. Makes sure he gets my sea sack. Promise me that. Fare yeh well, young 'un.'

'It's not too late,' I called after her. 'Take the rope.'

Her head ducked under, and she came up again, gulping. 'If yeh and yer friends ever win over the Morok, yeh need… to track Aehmir – he can 'elp – 'elp with it – with yer burden.' She pointed towards the bottom of the boat where the *papose* lay as she drifted away, head barely above water, the life leaking from her, the water turning dark red around her. 'I never meant to harm yeh, young 'un,' she cried in a voice that was barely a whisper. 'Tell Tiroc Og I'm sorry… that I failed yeh all – fer what I did.'

'Don't leave me!' I moaned in desperation, pulling on the mainsail stay, trying to bring the boat round towards her. But too late. She was gone.

The winds had died. The lake was calm.

I gazed mutely at the spot where I'd last seen her, now just a circle of bloody bubbles. Sorrow filled my heart, my rage against her vanished like the wind. She may have brought me to this terrible juncture, but in the end, she'd given her life to save mine.

I shook myself. I was becalmed and drifting aimlessly. I needed to find a way to get ashore. Thinking quickly, I used one of Romi's loose ropes to extend the stay on the foresail, then pulled it tight and dragged it towards the tiller. There was just enough wind to turn the boat back round. It started to drift towards the rim, very slowly, but purposefully, almost entirely of its own volition.

Out of nowhere, another Skarag, larger than the others, could be seen flying low across the water, heading straight for the *scud*, talons outstretched. I looked for my *papose*. It was out of easy reach, lying on the deck, separate from me, half under an oar as if in hiding. Inert. No intervention; no green flash or time shift. The creature was nearing, its huge wings covering the horizon, horrible yellow eyes fixed on mine.

The stink of it reached me first, then my whole world grew dark. I was in its shadow. Steeling myself for the impact, I stood erect, gripped Garidh's cutlass with both hands and readied myself to make one final thrust for my life.

I thought I'd given all I could. But it wasn't enough.

4

ON THE RIM

Involuntarily I'd shut my eyes. I heard the Skarag screech, make a choking gurgling noise and when I looked, saw it fall back, rise up and tumble backwards into the lake, a feather arrow embedded in its neck. I heard a shout and saw a stone dugout speeding towards the broken *scud*, Bran paddling at the fore, Tiroc Og standing upright, bow in one hand. 'Am I glad to see you!' I shouted.

'Another close 'un,' beamed Bran.

Tiroc Og was staring over my shoulder, his expression grim. I turned to follow his gaze and saw a flotilla of dark sails. The sheets were full, the wind strong, the boats coming straight for us. White water foamed at the skull shaped prows. The dugout drew up alongside. 'Get in quick,' urged Bran, grabbing the edge of the *scud*. I rummaged around for my weapons, found them bundled under some blankets, grabbed them, threw my *papose* over my shoulder, stowed Garidh's cutlass in my belt, clambered over and got between my friends.

'Grab a paddle,' said Bran, steering the dugout around. 'We needst get ashore quick.'

But as we began to drift away, I remembered Romi's pack. 'We have to go back,' I said. 'I've forgotten something – for you, Tiroc. It's important – a dying request from Romi.'

He nodded gravely, as if he knew what it was, reversing his paddling. We swept back round to the *scud*, already listing in the water, rudderless. I clutched its side, reached over and grabbed Romi's sea sack.

'Bran, get yer axe, hole thon thing,' Tiroc Og shouted. 'Osian, empty Romi's sack out here so we can take what we need. Then take anything of yers – like yer fur collar… anything else yeh can spare from yer *papose*. Stuff them into the sea sack. And somethin' heavy. Garidh's blade, that'd do. Put a tear down it.'

I did as I was told. 'Now throw 'em all over. Hurry!' he urged.

I launched the sea sack into the water. Half full of air, it floated in the swell, the lighter contents floating out. 'Now stick Bran's spear into thon thing.' He pointed to the floating corpse of the Skarag. 'Bran, paddle as close as yeh can.' Duly I stuck the spear deep into the corpse, recoiling at the stench as its blackish blood spilled out across the boat.

'Now throw it in and take up a paddle for our lives.'

Water was pouring into the *scud* through the holes Bran had made with his axe. It tilted forward, then rolled right over and began to sink. Romi's sea sack swirled in a circle of bubbles nearby. The dead Skarag had disappeared, its blood probably a magnet to the dreadful creature that had taken Garidh.

Leaving the scene of Romi's tragic end, we pushed towards the shore and quickly beached. Across the water the sails of the flotilla grew bigger, swelling in the full breeze, still too far away to make out any detail – equally unlikely that we could be seen. Dragging the dugout up the beach, we hid it behind a cluster of boulders then, crouching within a pile of driftwood debris, watched as the flotilla came into view, then headed straight for the *scud* – now drifting close to the shore, water pooling over its remaining sail.

Twilight was setting in, visibility getting poor, but I counted twelve craft in total, full size tri-masted *scud*, surrounding the collapsed boat. From one ship two stump boats were lowered into the water and using nets, the crews commenced to sweep up the flotsam I'd thrown in. Romi's half sunken *scud* dropped below the surface, then disappeared. A tall, cloaked figure standing on the foredeck seemed to be examining the rescued flotsam, discarding bits and cursing with frustration. It was the Ferok in the jay coloured body mail I'd first seen in the ruins of Iteron and under Romi's treehouse. Though I couldn't make out the eye patch, I had little doubt who it was. 'Krachter!' I exclaimed.

'I'm hopin' they'll think its yeh and thon thing gone below, Osian. They won't go divin' in these waters.'

I shuddered, thinking of the creature that had taken Garidh.

The ships of the flotilla tacked round and began to make way back where they'd come. It looked like they'd given up. Could it be a ruse? Or had they given up – assumed we'd all come to a tragic end?

I asked Tiroc Og about the rest of the company. He explained all were safe and well, encamped in a lava hollow under the shadow of the crater rim. 'Talk later,' he murmured as we began to head back, the shifting pebbles making for tricky walking.

When we arrived at the hollow I was warmly greeted by the others, seated on rocks round a well-concealed driftwood fire and eating.

My gaze fell on Gimin, her mane bright red in the firelight, her eyes twinkling like stars. She smiled at me and I smiled back, but at that moment Bron clapped me on the back – hard! ''ungry, Albin?' he asked. 'Very,' I replied, glancing back at Gimin. But she'd looked away. Bron had prepared a stew of dried fish simmered in herbs, to be eaten with oatcakes. Either his cooking had improved, or my appetite was such that anything I ate tasted marvellous. My share was consumed in seconds.

After I'd eaten, Tiroc Og took me to one side and asked me to tell him everything that had occurred during my captivity. Sitting with my back to a rock, my fur pulled around my shoulders against the chilly night mist, I relayed the extraordinary sequence of events since I'd been taken, as well as everything I'd overheard or been told by Romi.

None of it seemed to particularly surprise him. He nodded from time to time, tapping his pipe out on a stone, refilling and relighting it. When I described how Romi had died I was sure I saw a glint of moisture in his eyes.

'I will tell yeh of Romi,' he said. 'The old she-fox and I had a long friendship despite some friction between our clans. Her tribe, the Tarsin, were at one time just pirates, bloodthirsty critters roaming the seas and living off booty and the labours of others. But when their numbers disappeared into the sea mists, them that were left took to livin' on the land. Romi's own clan lived peaceably in the forests when not mastering sea ships fer Aguan merchants. When the Morok came, we took to the woods and she and the other Tarsin helped us by spyin' on them from the treetops and warnin' us of their movements. From the tree tops they can see for many leagues, an' can move like birds across the forests.'

'It was her then that followed me just when I arrived at the river. Those conch calls were hers – yours?'

'Yes. We didn't know who yeh were an' what yeh were up to – and in these times…'

'She was one of you. But she betrayed you.'

Tiroc Og paused for a moment, then said, 'My heart is soft with forgiveness for an old friend who'd been trapped – despite what she did.'

Then, I remembered the stuff from her sea sack I'd bundled together from the bottom of the dugout into my *papose*. I fished it out. 'I'd almost forgotten. She asked me to give you this.'

He took the bundle, casually put it to one side and re-lit his pipe, almost as if he already knew what was in there. It was one of those moments where I felt, once again, that I was only getting a part picture of things; there was more to his relationship with the old She-Tarsin than met the eye.

I said, 'Tell me, Tiroc Og, how was it that I was taken – that you were so misled by the Aguan – allowed Garidh to betray us?'

'Ah, young un',' he replied with a wry smile. 'We were tricked there fer sure. The gas was among us afore we could react. They caught us off-guard, to my shame. But we'd never been fooled by the Aguan, Garidh. Like most of his tribe, they'll change sides for the highest bidder. I thought it useful to have such as him among us.'

'What do you mean?' I exclaimed, flabbergasted. 'He was a spy – and you knew it. The Morok knew our whereabouts – and now they know what you're planning!'

'I'll tell yeh, young 'un,' he said, laughing. 'He only knew what we wanted him to know and the harriers have been keeping sharp eyes on their movements. The night following the taking of Trisuldur, Garidh was spotted leaving camp – evading the watch. Ganoc tracked him to a clearing in the woods where he spied him tying a scroll to the leg of thon eagle of Krachter's.'

'What?! Ganoc didn't try to stop him – or the eagle? What about the other one – Aridh?' I urged. 'Is he a spy too? He's missing.'

'Ah. I sent him to Cana-Din's camp in the Terai, with a message – about the meeting place.'

I stared at him, mouth gaping. 'You trust *him*?'

He laughed. 'Yer young, Osian, and don't know how battles are lost and won; more than half of it is like the squirrels do, second-guessing the enemy's moves – just like in a game of *skim*. Krachter and Kahl are not easily fooled and have spies everywhere, so we keeps feedin' them mixed signals, mos'ly false destinations fer our movements, our meeting places and how we get to Rakhaus.'

'Your trust surprises me. I'd always been wary of Aridh. But, oddly, never Garidh. And what about Romi?'

'Well, she was indeed one of us – a kind of rear watch. Aridh, believe it or not, is with us. He has a life debt with me and,' he paused, 'knows he'll be well rewarded. He kept us informed about everything Garidh was up to. And even if Aridh switches sides now, nothing is lost.'

'Romi said the Morok had Kami and were threatening a terrible torture. Yet, she gave her life for me in the end.'

'Yes. We saw it all from the rim,' he said, a catch in his throat. 'They surprised us with the sleeping gas, for certain. Garidh could have killed us, after all – but Romi wouldn't have allowed that. When we woke we tracked yeh to the rim – saw yer god stone, then the *scud* out on the water.'

A sudden breeze came up, causing the fire to flicker and roll. The night mist had cleared but the darkness was complete. Everything was black – the sky, the boulders and the beach – and taking all this in, where we were and what terrors lay ahead, I had a sudden awful sense of how our world might end, in thrall to forces of darkness. Yet, I reasoned, I and my companions had made it this far without loss. Here, now, we were alive – brothers and sisters on the rim of night, but with a new day to come – and despite the odds, I had to hope and pray it would be ours.

Later, wrapped in my blanket near to the fire, I lay watching the light of the flames flicker on the rocks and the diligent faces of the night watch, perched on boulders above us. Tiroc Og was sat alone by the fire in his usual contemplative position: cross-legged, pipe in his mouth, staring into the embers.

Seeing me awake, he spoke softly. 'Osian, yeh told me before yer kin had gone with two Aguan on their pilgrimage.'

'Yes.'

'And you saw them set out? Have yeh considered that one of 'em guards might have been Aguan friend, Garidh?'

'What?' I bolted upright; all thoughts of sleep forgotten. I never saw their faces. 'What are you thinking?'

'That Garidh had been paid to capture yer kin, take them somewhere to be collected by the Morok to be brought to Rakhaus.'

'What interest could he possibly have in my family?'

'I've been asking myself the same question – trying to un-weave the strings of the web that involved yeh being here – and with that...'

'The *Solon*?'

'Yes. The Norns – the Fates – don't move by chance. There's always an order to the way things...'

'What do you mean?'

'Some kind of connection 'tween yer family and the Morok – Kahl, even.'

'That makes no sense.'

'Yeh say. But sometimes these things go deeper, further back in the mists than we think – or more likely, can know of.'

'What kind of connection do you mean, Tiroc Og?'

'That we've yet to find out – if indeed there's anything in it, unless it's meant to be mystery known only to the Norns.'

My tribe did believe in past lives – that everything living had been on the earth before. And of course, belief in fate – in things prescribed – and the angels of fate, the Norns, was common. But I was always thought these ideas were like ghosts and bogles. Fantasies for the innocents.

'There's also the fact of the *Solon* finding yeh, Osian,' Tiroc Og continued.

'Finding me? I'm sorry. Now you are speaking in riddles.'

'Well, why did it come to yeh? Why not any of the rest of us?'

I stared at him, still puzzled.

He chuckled – no doubt at the expression on my face. "Tis long believed by all the *Akari* – shamans like me – that nothin' in life happens by chance. And if yeh takes thon tack, it's not so hard to believe, Osian, that there's some feathery bond – or something like it – 'atween the *Solon*, yer kin and old Gwion-Din, fer 'em to take him as well.'

I remained puzzled. 'So how do I come into this?' I queried.

'Gwion-Din knew yeh were coming?'

'My grandfather will have passed word to Gwion-Din to let him know I was coming. But that doesn't mean anything.'

Tiroc Og smiled in response. So I persisted. 'What possible connection could there be between between us all – if you say my finding it was not just chance?'

'Some link, that existed before yeh ever set eyes on it, going back into the mists of the moons. This is known to Kahl, and that'll be why he wants yeh – not dead, but alive! He's a skryer, remember, can see into moons and winters past and dimly into those to come. Yer kin might well have been lured into his keeping – as a caution against the problems he saw lying ahead.' Then, pointing at my *papose*, he said, 'The strange fact of yeh ending up with the *Solon* was no coincidence. It went outside his control and worse, ended up in the possession of yeh of all people. The ferry sinking was no accident. The Solon sought you out. And at least now, no doubt, he can use yer kin as ransom.'

I shivered, my head reeling. The very idea of my kin being involved in some kind of bizarre intrigue was beyond my comprehension. But then I'd never fully understood why they'd journeyed when they did, going to Erainn when they did. Was there something more to this than met the eye? Had they been summoned – or drawn into a trap? As for Grandfather, there had always been so much mystery about his first visit to Erainn, the journey he never talked of. But surely all this was just too fanciful. I shook my head in disbelief.

'I never thought,' Tiroc Og said, almost reading my mind, 'that yer kin were really embarking on some kind of pilgrimage. ''Tis not that I don't believe *yeh*, Osian. It's just when they set out, the Morok had already overran Erainn. The Aguan they went with would have known that for certain.'

'I've always puzzled over this myself,' I said.

'Yeh are yet young in the ways of the world – and know not of the hidden forces that lie behind what we do, where we go.'

I just shrugged. After what I'd witnessed so far on my journey, and my strange bond with the *Solon* I could almost believe in anything, even this.

'Anyways,' he continued. 'Garidh was the last to join our company – of course I never trusted him. I knew he was a spy from the outset, so I decided to play him to our advantage. Meantime, I'm hoping that Krachter thinks both yeh and the *Solon* are at the bottom of Krater Lake, never to be returned to the light. Kahl may well doubt that – but it's useful to us if in the meantime Krachter thinks yeh are both lost, that his plan with Romi went so badly wrong.'

'You mean your ruse with sinking the boat.'

'But Krachter knows though *we* are out here – and that we'll be coming.'

I drew breath, trying to digest all this. I'd been brought up a simple hunter and fisher. This curious world of watching and spying, of intrigue and deception, double-crossing and trickery was all new to me. As for my kin to have been involved in any such intrigues still seemed unlikely – other than as victims. As for Grandfather. Well, there was so much about him that was a mystery to all, that you just never knew.

Tiroc Og lay back and pulled his blanket up to his chin. But my mind was racing. I wasn't ready for sleep. 'So, what now, Tiroc Og?

Given all you've told me, all you know – what are we now going to do? What do you think the Morok will do?'

At this he sat up and leaned on an elbow, frowning into the fire. 'I'll tell yeh. I'm hopin' the Morok will believes some kind of invasion force will arrive on the western shores of Rakhaus. It's rocky, marsh and inhospitable but not impossible for tribes such as ours – and they know this. If so, if I was him, I'd put the bulk of his army on that side and put the sailin' *scuds* on the water out of reach of our arrows. It's certainly what I'd do, usin' the lines I've fed 'em through the Aguan.'

'And if they do this it plays into yer hands, I take it?'

He nodded and smiled grimly. 'Once on the west they won't be able to move quickly to any other part of the island.'

'Have you heard from Cana-Din?' I asked, fearing that without whatever forces she could muster, even the most cunning of Tiroc Og's carefully laid plans would probably founder.

'No. But she knows what to do in any event – if she can carry it out.'

I was little the wiser. 'What about us, then? Where – how – do we get to on Rakhaus?'

He yawned. 'It was never my plan to for us enter Rakhaus by land or water.'

'Why, then, Tiroc Og?' I spluttered in amazement. 'Why carry all those dugouts all this way?'

He laughed. 'Of course – you don't know,' he said. 'Taking the dugouts all the way was a ruse; highly visible to watchin' eyes.' He pointed upwards. Krachter's flying spies had probably seen us climbing Kariyag and for all I know, seen the company crossing over the rim. Though I hadn't seen the eagle when we were scuppering Romi's *scud*, that didn't mean that those keen eyes weren't watching. But, going to all that trouble with the dugouts, really?

'A ruse, you say?'

'We won't use them to get to Rakhaus, but we'll scupper some – for show!'

My jaw dropped. 'How do we get there, then – fly?'

Laughing, he replied, 'We'll enter Rakhaus, my friend, from the very last place they'd expect.'

'Where's that?'

'From the inside.'

5

THE TUNNEL

Tiroc Og was gone from the fireside when I woke. He returned as we broke fast – another of Bron's fishmeal porridges with oatcakes. The preparations were nothing like Drion's but warming and enlivening nonetheless; and for once we had second helpings. From this I took that we would be journeying without halts. But dawn was breaking. Were we really going to travel in open daylight?

Breaking camp, we followed Tiroc Og to a rough boulder circle close to the crater rim. 'This, I think, is the one,' he said, poking at some pebbles with his stick in the middle of the ring. Then, getting to his knees he scraped away an area of black sand and revealed a grey-black flagstone, roughly circular in shape. 'Yes, just as it was,' he muttered, digging his fingers under an edge. 'Here, Bran, Bron – one of you either side.'

His lieutenant pushed the brand beneath the flagstone revealing a passage below, with steps carved into the black rock leading down into darkness. A stairway beneath a beach! It hardly seemed credible, but then, so much of what I'd seen on my extraordinary journey was unlikely – my long-held scepticism about monsters, ghosts, magic and gods had already been shattered, now an aberration in nature! None of the others seemed surprised at this curious wonder. Then, little about their wily chief ever came as a shock.

On a word from him, two of the pumice dugouts were holed and pushed into the lake shallows by the Barod, where they half sank into the mud. Then various items were thrown into the water: a couple of broken spears, some well-worn blankets and furs, some sacking and, I noticed, a bag of (presumably) stale food and a few wooden cooking utensils.

A light wind quickly dispersed the debris, sending our abandoned belongings far out into the lake. A piece of extra trickery by Tiroc Og, no doubt. Krachter's eagle – or any Skarag – spotting this stuff might believe the renegades had tried to cross and failed – taken below, like me and the *Solon*, by the monsters of the deep.

Later, with Ganoc leading, we clambered easily in single file down through the tunnel entrance. Bran and Yamis came last, dragging down the surviving dugouts then replacing the flagstone. After an *hora* or so we reached the bottom where it levelled out into a cavernous, tube-like tunnel, its sloping floor bone dry, littered with grey dust and cobwebs. In the light of the firebrand, it looked like we were in the digestive tract of some creature and, Tiroc Og explained, that in one way it really was – the innards of an exploded earth monster – a volcano. We were walking deep inside a mountain! The air was warm but had a sulphurous smell like the hot mountain pools at home.

'We know of three such tunnels with hidden entrances into Rakhaus,' he said to me as he led the way. 'Legend has it they were used by the fire dragons of Ragnaroc – the last days of the ancient world – when they roared out of Fire Mountain to take vengeance on the Manu for poisoning their habitat.'

'How did you know about them – the tunnels?' I asked.

'During my shaman's apprenticeship, my teacher and I visited Elvintal as guests of the monks, staying in the monastery for one whole winter. We crossed under the water using this very one.'

'Your teacher. Ah. Who was that?' I politely queried.

'One of the Wind Hare.'

'Wind Hare?' The foreteller in a tale, told me by a forester at the start of my journey that predicted the demise of the Marcher Lords of Erainn, was of that tribe. And of course, the little book of sayings in my *papose* was written by a Wind Hare with the name in him of Aehmir.

'Yes, only a few about.'

'Grandfather knew one. He gave me a little book of his teachings. I have been studying them on my travels.'

Tiroc Og paused in his step and turned to face me. 'Really, Osian?' he said. 'What was the name in him – yer grandfather's friend?'

'Aehmir is the name on the book: "Ayh – meer" I think its pronounced.'

'Ha! The very one. Old Aehmir helped my father and yer grandfather when they helped bring about the peace of the Marsh wars. He became my teacher – brought me here.'

I remembered Romi's mention of the name. 'Romi, before she died – she said I needed to find an Aehmir. That he'd know about the *Solon* – what I was to do with it. Is it the same?'

'Of course, of course,' Tiroc Og muttered, continuing his stride forwards. 'Yes, he might, he well might...' Nodding thoughtfully, as if storing this bit of information from Romi away, he continued, 'Aehmir, and it'll be same, knew of the secret tunnels from the monks.'

'Won't the Morok know about them?'

'The monks left these parts before the Morok arrived, so they'll have no means of knowing. Kahl, I know, for some reason has a particular hatred for the Lepoch – the Wind Hare. His Ferok scoured all of Manau for any that survive, but as far as I knows never found any – and old Aehmir is too cunning to be caught by such as them.'

I thought of the little book of sayings I'd been reading and found it easy to imagine many reasons why they and their wisdoms would be so hateful to the Morok. "*There is no greater good for a warrior than to fight in a righteous war,*" Aehmir had said. But then, didn't all warriors think their war was righteous? Maybe the Morok did, too?

'Where are the other tunnels?' asked Bran.

'One runs from the edge of Lake Mantarowar in the far Westerlands under the frozen marshes and comes out on Rakhaus into the old Elvintal prayer room. The third is the largest and strangest of all. There's a hidden maze of flagstones on a small Arctos island between Manau and Skraelandia leading to a huge tunnel that runs deep under the Broken Sea then into the heart of Kariyag, before coming up into the middle of the island. The monks believed it was once used as a mine shaft by the Manu to take out quartzes and moonsilver. It's so big, an army of thousands could pass through. 'Tis my belief, my hope, the Morok know none of this – these.'

'Cana-Din? She'll be coming through that one?'

He shrugged. 'That is my hope and prayer.'

'If none of that happens, would we be going in without her? No invasion?'

'What cannot be done by force, can be attempted by guile. The Krol robes we took from Trisuldur will allow three of our number to enter Elvintal in disguise, the others to wait at the tunnel entrance for my signal. They are well provided and the air in the tunnel is good. If we don't make contact within three nightfalls, they must assume the worst, head for the Terai and join up with our other fighters. There will be another day – many battles in a war such as this. Not all will be like the victory at Trisuldur.'

The shy Brach, Hakon, who'd been walking immediately behind us, spoke up. 'I've 'eard this, Chief. Tis surely madness to separate,' he said. 'We shoulds all go in t'gether, die t'gether if needs be, jes as we 'ave lived n' fought t'gether.'

'I am grateful for yer words, bold Hakon,' replied Tiroc Og, 'but should our mission fail, there must be some of us left to lead other fighters agin' the Morok.'

'But after us,' said Hakon, 'there'll be few left t'carry on the fight. The Eronn 'ave mosly been enslaved, murdered or starved. The Wildcat, Barod an' others are too few or too scattered. And we Brach and Sideag outcastes are thin on the ground. This may be our last chance t' bloody 'em.' His words echoed back and forwards around the tunnel, making it seem like there was not just one Hakon, but many.

'Do yeh Hakon speak for all, all who have no kin in Rakhaus?'

'Aye, Tiroc Og, that I do, we mus' try to kill Krachter, free the slaves,' he replied. A clamour of shouts followed from all down the line, the echoing voices from all making it feel as if we already had an army in place. Tiroc Og smiled warmly. I saw the moisture in his eye.

We were now making swift progress through the tunnel, now wider than before. Tiroc Og turned and said to me, ''Tis true that if Cana-Din gets the Easter tribes aboard, this guarantees the help of the Wester tribes, the Ruadh and the Rigead, the Red Fox and Red Wolf and the others. The dog tribes in particular are powerful and numerous, even if, present friends esceptin', they haven't yet declared against the Morok. They won't want to be left out of any campaign against a common enemy – certainly not let their cousins in the east get all the glory of victory. And Reyn, he of the Red Fox has no love for the invaders. One day he'll be chief, and along with the chief of the Rideag in command of the largest tribe in all Erainn, greater than the Brach and the Sideag combined.'

'Reyn!' I chipped in. 'Reyn was the first traveller I met on my journey – on the edge of the Karst. We were attacked by Starag, but he fought them off. He was going to a gathering of the western clans.'

'Yes. I remember yeh telling me. Thon gathering was to talk over the Morok threat. Kahl has always exploited the age-old enmities and rivalries 'atween the tribes for his ends. He's had envoys – Krol – attendin' both camps. This I know. But the great chiefs of the east and west have to pull together. They needs to know that the Morok devils won't stop till the whole of Manau, including their territories, is theirs.'

Bran caught my eye, nodded and smiled thinly. Were he chief of the Brach, in place of his aged father, I knew, things would be different – not tomorrow, but now!

Hakon, Bran's cousin, still walking close behind but now in company with Bran, muttered agreement to what he was hearing. Tiroc Og turned to him, saying, 'Ah brother Hakon. If we don't return, yeh must go back to Clachoile. Seek the counsels of yer chief. Tell him what yeh have seen, what yeh know – and urge him to support Cana-Din. Yeh'll have friends surely among the Sideag – whom the Morok fear the most – who can talk to their chief. Seek them out. Ah – there's Ranig too,' he added, seeing that fearsome warrior close behind Bran and Hakon.

Ranig was the only Sideag, Grey Wolf, in the group. He also spoke up. 'Brave Tiroc Og, I say this: likes Amon of the Brach, our chief, 'll only act if he sees 'tis in his interest – and if the Brach are already persuaded.'

'I've heard, Tiroc Og,' pitched in Bran. 'Both the big chiefs 'ave the counsel of one of 'em fork-tongued Krol sittin' by their campfires, telling of th' chests of sungolds and moonsilvers that are to be brought for them from across the Great Lake o' Risin' and Fallin' Water – if they come aboard for the Morok.'

'Treasure which they'll never see, of course,' replied Tiroc Og. 'For yeh, Hakon and all others cast out from their tribes, if we don't succeed, yeh must return to yer fold and help persuade 'em to act. This, then, would be yer destiny instead of a forgotten death on Rakhaus. It would be of this, many moons from now, the tribes will sing.'

To this Hakon seemed to assent with a simple bow, then retired behind us and quickly became involved in an animated conversation with Ranig. I'd been told that these two were great friends, sharing a life debt. They were the best spear and *aber-axe* fighters in the company, able to throw or fire their weapons prodigious distances.

***

The march through the tunnel took two full days. At the end of the first we had a welcome meal of salt fish and smoke-dried game roasted over charcoals and washed down with sparkling lightly sulphurous water drawn from a spring on the rim. On the second day we came to a series of pillars extended from floor to ceiling. Our firebrands illuminated rock forms savagely twisted and torn as if squeezed between the talons of some giant beast. Crystals in the rock, flakes of black mica and glassy green jet sparkled brightly in the gloaming. When I asked about them, Bran said, 'Aye. The legend says these were made when the dragons o' Ragnarok paused for breath.'

I was reminded of the cavern pillars in the Karst and the mention of dragons made me wonder if the Skarag were descendants of the fire-lizards of legend. The cavern in the Karst was where I'd first seen those horrid creatures. There also I'd come across the one Tiroc Og had called an earth dragon; where my journey into the night of the Morok had begun and where, of course, I'd had my first sighting of the *Solon*. I thought of our destination, of cavernous holes like the one we were crossing through like the one under the Sentinel, the insect-shaped hill where the Skarag had their lair.

'Does Rakhaus have places that look like this, Bran? Have you been there?' I asked with a wary glance at the evil looking gnarled pillars.

'No, not been there, so I don't know what's under it. All I knows about Rakhaus is that Kahl's lieutenant, resides in the old monastery wi' walls and tors fathoms thick. He's said to be like the devil his-self, wi' his huge red Ferok face and a patch o'er one eye. He does whatever his chief bids and no doubt plenty of stuff he's not bid to do too, so long as it's cruel. I'm told the hilt of his sword is Okwa bone and he keeps a dark bird on his arm to spy for 'im and message the Morok chief.'

I thought of my kin, being held with Kami and others in the Ferok's wicked grip, possibly being tormented. I simmered with rage, an anger I couldn't contain. I struck at a pillar with my staff, sending vibrations coursing through my body and an echo along the tunnel, causing everyone to glance my way.

Bran lightly touched my shoulder. ''Tis good to be angry, Osian. We've all got grievances against thon devils fer what they've done to our friends, but save yer stick fer breakin' Morok heads rather than old stones.'

I took a deep breath to calm myself.

'What is the size of the Morok force in Rakhaus – and elsewhere?' I asked, surprising myself that I didn't already know or couldn't remember this.

'Thousands in Rakhaus, I believes. Many's more, tens o' thousands, again in other places like the huge camp in the forest outside Erintor and the workcamps o' slaves edging the Broken Sea and in the far chasms o' Karinprayag where they mine black gold fer their fires and weapons forges.'

I could barely comprehend the scale of it all. My tribe – Albin Otar living south of the White Mountains, our homeland – numbered a mere few hundred, if that; and the settlements of our other local tribes, the earthen homes, tree houses and cave dwellings of the White Rhuad, Deer, Snake, Cougar and Crow, only housed a few clans of each. Alba wasn't rich like Erainn in hunting grounds and fields and our soils are thin and frozen half the year, so our numbers were never going to be huge. The total population of Alba couldn't amount to more than a few thousand souls, if that.

'Aye, there's some numbers o' them alright,' commented Bran, probably observing the surprise on my face. 'We're up against it, fer sure. But yeh knows what they say: the bigger the waterfall, the harder it bears down on the rocks below. Kahl's empire might jes' be built on a cliff edge that one day will get washed away, just as happened in the time of the Manu.'

'I hope you're right, Bran. I pray you're right.'

'Shhhsh,' came a whisper from the front.

From round a bend ahead came a rattling sound, faint at first but getting louder and with it, a strong smell of ordure and decay. Ganoc and Tiroc Og, swords drawn, led the way and we fell into a tight formation behind them as we all crept slowly forward.

Suddenly the tunnel was filled with flittering dark shapes all around us, darting here and there. I felt something brush past my face, the soft touch of a leathery wing. Then I heard laughter. The shapes vanished as quickly as they'd appeared and now everyone was on their feet, wiping away dust that had dropped onto our shoulders.

'Bats,' chuckled Bran, ducking as a couple of stragglers passed over his head, their wings zipping frantically with the effort to keep up.

''Tis a good sign,' said Tiroc Og, lowering his sword. 'We must be near an opening – tunnel's end.'

Passing the last pillars we arrived at the end of the tunnel. This was a wall of flattish stones, broken in parts, with some rough timber ladders at the base. Tiroc Og explained that this was a double wall between us and the cellars of Elvintal. Pointing to the stones, he said, 'These are dry laid stones, not mortared so they can be easily moved, but we must take care. We'll have to dismantle it starting at the top, as quiet as the baby deer, in case the Morok have discovered the labyrinth 'neath the old castle and are using the chambers for some horrible purpose.'

I drew breath as I realised the possibility of being so close to the enemy – incredibly, right inside or under their lair. But the *Solon* did not react in any way. If there were Morok on the other side waiting for us, they were not nearby.

The Barod checked and erected the ladders and started to lift away stones from the first wall, passing them down to one another then to the rest of us. Carefully, we piled them along the sides of the tunnel in a regular fashion. 'So's they can be easily replaced, stone fer stone,' Tiroc Og explained.

An opening was made in the wall with almost no sound and very little dust, revealing a second wall, again cracked in places, but still darkness beyond. We'd been working for well over a couple of *hora* before Tiroc Og whispered, 'Rations now.' There was a gleam of excitement in his eyes as he said it. 'Take water and rest afore we open this one up.' He peered through a gap in the stones of the interior wall. 'Jes beyond is Elvintal. Yahl be with us.'

We took our rations in silence. Tiroc Og sat a little way apart, taking items out of his long pack. I recognised Romi's bundle among them and watched with curiosity as he untied its knots and emptied the contents on the ground.

Picking over them he selected two cylindrical tubes, the smaller one green, the larger a cloudy blue. From the green one he pulled a tiny piece of paper which he peered at, then put to one side. The blue tube he placed gingerly into a leather pouch, which he tucked inside his robe. Making a cursory check of the other things, he re-tied them, then stood and carried the bundle back up the tunnel, lighting a twig from one of the firebrands as he passed. A little while later he could be heard chanting and a drift of scented smoke appeared and hung in the still air. For a second, I thought I caught the sound of water, like waves lapping on a shore. Tiroc Og, the shaman, was using the old She-Tarsin's belongings to send her spirit on its last voyage – over the seas to the stars. She was being blessed. And in that moment I thought there was something odd about her betrayal episode: as so many times before, more had been going on than met the eye. Or was this indeed Romi's destiny and there had been premonitions of some kind?

I gratefully accepted a second portion of dry rations from Bron and looked around at the others. The mood was sombre, yet their faces showed only calmness, a quiet anticipation. Gimin, her eyes glinting in the light of the firebrand, caught my gaze and smiled broadly. I began to rise, to go towards her, but seeing me she shook her head and looked to the ground.

Feeling a little put out I sat back down, but when I looked again, she was grinning and mouthing 'Wait, talk later.' Then, 'There will be time.' I smiled back, a gentle unfamiliar tingling spreading over my body.

I felt a nudge in my ribs. It was Bran, grinning at me. 'Wake up, Osian, listen.'

I saw that Tiroc Og had already returned and was softly speaking: ''Tis time, brothers and sisters. We mus' take down a small part of thon wall,' adding with a smile, 'just enough for a Brach to go through.'

A hole was quickly made and the light of a single firebrand showed a dusty empty space beyond with well-crafted curved stones laid end to end. A metal ladder ran up the far side.

''Tis a dry well,' whispered Tiroc Og. 'My teacher Aehmir told me the old ones used such as these to ferment *soma* to make offerings to the gods. This one lies 'neath the hearthstone of a prayer hall – once the heart of Elvintal. What's up there now, I don't know. But in this place, wherever any of us now go, the *sidhe* of the old ones – those who were here before – will be with us. They too 'ill want vengeance on the devils that have been desecrating their sacred place.' Then, mounting one of the loosed boulders, he turned and spoke aloud. 'Listen close, brothers. I and two companions will go forward and scout where Gwion-Din and the others are being held and return to collect yeh. Meantime, rest, eat, prepare yer weapons and be ready. But...' he paused. 'If we haven't returned by two nightfalls, Yeh mus' go back to the forests. Find Cana-Din. Join her band. Only she can take on the might of Kahl and his sorcery. The future of the free tribes lies not with me, but with her alone.'

'I will go with you,' said Lakon, raising his staff, followed by a clamour of voices as everyone else volunteered.

'Lakon, yeh cannot go. I need yeh and Ganoc to lead our brothers and sisters safely away. Death or capture in this place would be needless, a waste. Remember this. I hold you all equally dearly but respect my choice of companions fer this part of our mission. It has purpose.'

Lakon nodded respectfully and stepped back. Tiroc Og took a deep breath. 'My thanks, brother. Those who will go with me are two. There must be three with Bran... and the young Albin. Osian. We will enter Elvintal disguised in the Morok robes we took before, hoods up to hide our faces.'

There was a gasp when my name was announced. Around me I saw faces turning to stare; I saw disappointment, but no signs of disapproval. Whatever Tiroc Og's thinking was, they accepted it, such was the trust in their chief.

I couldn't believe nor understand why I had been chosen. I felt the hairs on my arms prickle with the thrill of it. But still I felt I had to say, 'I am honoured, Tiroc Og, but I'm the least experienced of all. I fear in coming with you I offend my fellows. You must go with another and I... I will follow – alone.'

'No. That would be foolhardy. Anyway, yeh have that which may be of use in our endeavours. Bran who will watch yer... our backs – and he has the knowledge of the firelogs.'

Some of the warriors murmured. Was it about the *Solon*? They had seen strange things with me. What did they know?

'Brothers, sisters. Are we together in this?'

Around me heads were nodding, but I could see glum faces. Among the younger warriors I saw tears. Gimin's face was lowered. I couldn't see her reaction. I looked at her, thinking we still hadn't the opportunity to talk, to get to know one another. Now, would we ever? I looked into other faces I had hardly known for any time yet knew already as dear friends.

I saw Bron gave Bran a sharp shove. There were tears in his eyes. I read from that we were not expected to return.

'Ganoc, the Ferok gowns and pack covers, please,' said Tiroc Og.

We donned the Morok robes. They smelt musty and rotten. Someone had cut the robes to our sizes, using the cut-offs to make Bran's bigger. The remnants were sheaths for our packs – cleverly woven together with furs like to the packs I'd seen Morok troopers carrying, complete with leather staff holsters. Bran explained that the sheaths would leave our hands free for get our weapons, which we'd have to tuck into our waist-belts under the robes. Unfortunately, we'd have to leave our own bows and crossbows behind, as they'd mark us out as enemy. In their place we were given looted Morok crossbolts and quivers which we slung over our shoulders. Tiroc Og's longbow was thin enough to fit under his robe, slung at his back. All in all, we looked the part, so long as our tell-tale features remained deep inside the big hoods.

All too soon it was the moment of parting. As we clambered into the hole, I was sure I heard a muted sob. This sent tears streaming down my face and I made no effort to wipe them away.

They replaced the stones from the other side. As the last one went in, I glimpsed Lakon, forcing a smile. 'The great Yahl go with you, brothers.' Standing behind him was Gimin, long red mane falling around her lovely face, her cheeks glistening with salt tears.

My heart ached. I wondered then if I'd ever see her – or any of them – again.

6

THE TOR OF DOORS

We clambered up the metal ladder: Tiroc Og leading, then me, then Bran. Bits of rust crumbled away from the sides, but the bars were firm and held, though they creaked under Bran's huge weight. Our Morok robes stretched to below the knee and the hidden weapons hindered easy movement. Worse was the stink of the cloth, a coarse fabric of goat hair, the smell of the enemy – a strange intimacy. But I'd get used to it!

From the last bar we scrambled out on to a ledge that positioned underneath a large grey flagstone. Tiroc Og sparked a thin firestick and poked at the edges of the stone with his Morok staff, bringing down a fine layer of dust and dusty cobwebs onto our heads.

''Tis a good sign,' he said. 'Shows the flagstone hasn't been disturbed. Better, even. For spiders to be in there means it's not been sealed. Now, help me move these,' he added, pointing to a pile of stones at the back of the ledge.

We dragged the stones underneath the stone to form a little hillock to get us nearer. Bran was first up and began to push the stone upwards.

'Just a little way, on the left edge first,' Tiroc Og cautioned. 'Bran, tell me what you see.' He turned to me. 'Osian, stand a little way back and aim yer bow at the gap.'

Bran heaved with his shoulder on the flag, unleashing more debris, until a tiny slice of light showed through. He pushed again, and the gap widened enough for him to look out. 'Nuthin' here, Chief. All's empty. Shall I go up?'

'Yes,' replied Tiroc Og, dampening the firestick. 'I'll follow. Osian, keep ready with yer bow. Shoot anyone that appears from above.'

Bran lifted the stone, slid it to the right and shoved his great frame through the opening. 'Wait,' he whispered back. 'Somethin's moving, I'm goin to look' and disappeared.

We hovered for what seemed an eternity, my hands getting numb from holding the armed crossbow. Still silence from above. Then, just when I felt I could bear it no longer, Bran's head appeared over the hole and he said with a grin, 'Yeh can put thon thing down, Osian. False alarm, only some rats, big 'uns though. Sorry fer the wait, brothers. Up yeh both come.' He reached down to haul us up.

Once through we pushed the stone back into place and I stood gazing into a dusty cavernous hall, stinking of rodent droppings. Soft grey light came in from three slit windows to one side, the frames spread with spiderweb-like silken tapestries. Fixed to the walls were tall totem staffs, elaborately carved with images of the spirit ancestors of the tribes: wolves and bears, hawks, foxes, deer, horses and beavers; every four-legged creature under the sun. The carvings were beautiful, scarily lifelike, as if they might pounce on us at any moment.

Tiroc Og caught my gaze. 'This is as it was, in my time here,' he said. 'Here the holy ones used to gather for day prayers. The poles were carved by the Wind Hare, but the walls, the stonework, are from before the coming of our ancestors. Manu maybe. None of our tribes build like that. The hall isn't used probably 'cos the Morok would think it cursed. They'd fear the ghost spirits locked inside the poles. Beyond there,' he gestured towards a large doorway strewn with webs, 'is where we go. This is one of the three towers of Elvintal, the Tor of Doors, where were all the monks sleeping cells. There's stairwells everywhere. So many rooms and halls and doors. If our friends are here, they'll most likely be kept in the cells above us.'

We began towards the doorway, our steps sounding dry and hollow in the silence, dust rising from our feet as we walked. Suddenly, the *Solon*, quiescent so far, sent a cold wave up my spine. A faint rattle came from the other side of the door, like keys jangling. I touched Tiroc Og's arm. He sniffed the air, pulled out his sword and nodded at Bran who did the same. I already had my hand on mine.

We waited. But no-one entered.

Tiroc Og sniffed again and shrugged. The warning at my back faded.

'It's gone, whatever it was,' I said.

'Probably just someone passing by,' Tiroc Og said, tentatively poking at the cobwebs that criss-crossed the doorway. 'Let me know if yeh hears anything else.'

Deep within the frame was a wooden door, but roughly hewn – in sharp contrast to the intricate stonework and fine carvings in the hall. 'Stay ready,' Tiroc Og whispered. 'This wasn't here in my time. The devils may have put it here to cut off this room.' He pondered for a moment, then said, 'Bran, lever the edge with your sword.'

Bran applied himself to the task. Grey light slipped through the gap he'd made. With one swift move he lifted the door from its hinges and put it to one side, going through first, sword at the ready. Tiroc Og and I followed, suppressing sneezes from the cloud of dust our feet kicked up. The space beyond was pitch dark and smelt of sweat. Bran replaced the door, pulling cobwebs across the frame to mask where we'd come through.

Two winding stairwells were ahead. From one came a buzzing, snorting sound. At my back the *Solon* quivered. Tiroc Og whispered, 'Stay close, listen to my breathing.'

In the darkness we crept up the stair where the buzzing came from, feeling for the edges of the spiral steps with our toes and running our fingers around the walls. Soon we came to a corridor with a faint red flickering light at one end, illuminating some shapes low to the ground. When nothing moved, we crept forward, crossbows armed.

The light was from a dying firebrand mounted on the wall. Two figures could be seen, half-sitting, half-lying against a door, detritus at their feet, cups lying on their sides and an upright flagon. They were snoring loudly, a strong smell of *aki* in the dank air. Bran went forward soundlessly and in two swift movements took their lives as they slept. The act seemed cold and cruel. But mercy of any kind was not an option now. Were we discovered, we were dead, our mission doomed. Covering his nose, Bran turned the bodies over and with a grunt held up a bunch of iron keys.

'Warders?' Tiroc Og mouthed. 'Prison guards?' Fingering his chin, he whispered, 'Bran, sit them back up against the wall. Put their knives in their mitts. Make it look like they had a fight to the death.'

It was quickly done, and as a finishing touch Bran kicked over the flagon, greenish *aki* mixing with the pool of dark blood. I felt my stomach clutch.

'That way is west – wrong side of the tower,' Tiroc Og said, pointing towards a doorway at the far end of the corridor. For a moment he looked uncertain – an unfamiliar expression on his usually calm face, then lifting the firebrand off the wall, said, 'We needs go easterly, then up. I'm hopin' that's the right way,' and muttered, 'so many doors, so many stairs…'

We came to a massive door dotted with metal studs, built to withstand an earth tremor by the look of it and intricately carved like the totems we'd seen in the prayer hall. It was locked but opened easily with the biggest of the keys Bran had taken, revealing an empty hallway with two more openings on the far wall.

As we went through, the *Solon* began to quiver. I caught hold of Tiroc Og's arm. We immediately backed off into the darkness, hands on swords and knives, facing the open door. Tiroc Og extinguished the firebrand as a light appeared beyond the door, casting long shadows on the wall: two figures. One limped behind the other, struggling to keep up. Keys jangled at his waist, rattling with his halting movements. Both were Ferok, unhooded. One carried a firebrand. They strode straight past us, talking quickly, their voices echoing in the corridor. The *Solon* vibrated with the sound of their voices, began turning their jagged incomprehensible speech into words inside my head.

''Ee wants some of 'em moved,' said the lead one.

I touched Tiroc Og's arm and pointed to my ears. 'I understand them,' I mouthed, hoping he could see my face in the gloom.

He stiffened a little, but not, I thought, with surprise, and rested a hand on my shoulder. I knew he feared the *Solon's* hold on me, its sorcerous powers. This was more evidence to him of those curious powers! But neither he nor I could deny its usefulness – for the present.

'Where to this time?' asked the other Ferok wearily.

'Out o' reach. Up to the Glassin Floor. Says there's rumours o' an attack,' came the reply.

'An attack? Fiddlesticks.'

''Tis not fer laughin', Kruc. Says there's a rebel army comin'. Ee's moved 'is largest forces to the wester marshes, jes' in case. And ee's set traps fer any that comes cross the lake from the south. And put the *scud* fleet there too.'

'Ha! 'Ow then are these rebels goin' to attack Rakhaus – from the air?'

'Nuthin' to laugh about,' grunted the lead Ferok, irritably. 'Anyways, we're to do it quickly, so hurry up there, stops dawdlin'.'

''Tis me leg,' groaned the other, halting suddenly, keys rattling to a stop. 'Yeh go ahead, I'll catch up.'

They disappeared through a door. It clanged shut behind them, closing off the light. But there were no sounds of locking.

I told Tiroc Og what I'd heard, but he'd already got the gist of it. I remembered he'd told me once that he'd made a point of learning bits of their dialect – from an Eronn rescued from a Morok slave encampment and as rescued by Cana-Din.

'Our young Albin has a useful skill, Bran,' Tiroc whispered. 'He can understand what the devils are saying.' Bran shot a quick glance at me, his eyes narrowing, then shrugged and nodded.

'We follow thon two,' Tiroc said. 'But this part of Elvintal's a real maze. We needst mark a route for our return.'

Bran reached into his robe, pulled out three tiny black pebbles, a souvenir maybe from the Lava Woods, aligned them roughly by the edge of the doorframe and kicked dust and webs over them.

We crept into the hall and up to the door through which the Ferok had disappeared. Tiroc Og eased it open and beckoned us forward. Up ahead I glimpsed one of the Ferok rounding a corner. His companion, stumbling far behind and out of the sight of the other, suddenly turned to look our way. Tiroc Og fired instantly. His victim crumpled to a heap with a low groan, an arrow deep in his back.

'Bran,' Tiroc Og whispered, 'yeh know what to do.'

Bran padded down the corridor and round the corner, then reappeared in mere seconds, dragging the other Ferok by a rope tight around the neck, gag over the mouth.

'What next, Chief?' he asked with a grim smile.

'Take the dead one back to the hall we came from. Sit 'im beside the others. Osian, help me drag this one over there.'

Taking an arm each, we hauled the Ferok into a recess in the wall, where with cord from his long pack, Tiroc Og tied his wrists and legs. When Bran returned, we released the rope from his neck. Then Bran slapped him across the face and laid the point of his knife at his throat. The Ferok winced, his eyes popping at the sight of the giant Brach's mouthful of broken teeth.

'Speak, dog,' whispered Tiroc Og in Ironese, taking out the gag, 'but cry out and the Brach will bite off yer tongue, blind yeh and let yeh die... slowly.'

'What d'yeh want?' gasped the Ferok in stilted Ironese, groaning and coughing for breath.

'Krachter has hostages: Gwion-Din the Fearsaig and an Albin, a smith, with an Eronn dam. Tell me where they're kept and we'll let you live.'

'Why shoulds I believes yeh?' spluttered the Ferok, his eyes darting between Bran, holding the knife to his throat and to Tiroc Og. 'If I tell yeh, yell kill me anyways.' Then, catching sight of me he suddenly began to shake uncontrollably, gibbering and slavering at the mouth just like I'd seen Romi on the boat squirming at the sight of my *papose*. It wasn't me, of course, but maybe what he thought I was carrying, that put the fear of Yahl into them. The *Solon*! I was its possessor; the very Albin the Morok were looking for. They knew I had something dangerous, sorcerous and their leader wanted it desperately – yet the Morok were terrified by it.

'My word's all that'll keep yeh alive,' said Tiroc Og. 'Yeh'll live beyond this day if yeh tells us the truth. If we find out yeh lied, Broken Teeth here'll come back and chew yer insides out – slowly.'

The Ferok continued to stare at me, shaking wildly. Bran slapped him again, drew the point of his knife lightly across our captive's throat then held its edge, bloodied from the scratch, against his left eye.

'Don't, don't!' the Ferok gasped. 'Keep thon devil away from me. The old Eronn dogs in the cell 'mmediately 'sides the courtyard, waitin' trial.'

'And the Albin smith – and the Eronn dam?'

The Ferok spluttered, 'The Glassin…' then began foaming at the mouth, staring at me, overwhelmed with terror, beyond speech.

Bran removed the knife. The Ferok slumped into unconsciousness. Questioning him further was useless. Tiroc Og pointed to the Ferok's sleeve and said, 'He'll be Krol, high priest, maybe…' On the hem were inlaid the three talons of the Morok inside a gold circle. It figured. Krol – Morok priests – would know what my possession had done to their fellows, what it could do to them. And it scared them more than the threat of death itself: victims of sorcery are condemned to eternal torture – they become the undead, *Katha*, half-lives locked in a terrifying world of shadows.

'Look at that,' I said, pointing to a black key dangling from a cord on the Ferok's chest. 'Thon thing round 'is neck. Could it be useful to us?'

'Take it, Osian. Yeh never know,' said Tiroc Og.

I cut the cord and held it up. It was heavy, iron, unusually long and thin, with the three-claw insignia of the Morok on the handle. As I put it inside my robe the *Solon* sent an icy wave up my back.

Sounds were coming from further up the corridor.

'Quickly, Bran, gag him again, in case,' whispered Tiroc Og. 'Stay in the shadows.'

We backed deep into the doorway, weapons at the ready. A black mastiff suddenly rushed past us, then came to a sudden stop, claws skittering on the stone floor, sniffed the air and growled. It knew we were there and was coming back. But slowly.

'Yer sling,' whispered Tiroc Og. I lifted it and began to cross the threshold. But as I moved the *Solon* shook wildly.

Suddenly, with a howl as if in pain, the dog shot away up the corridor. Then a troop of Morok ran past the doorway, seemingly unaware of our presence.

'Yahl preserves us,' whispered Tiroc Og. 'The dog knew we were here... yet...' He stared at me, thinking the same. It had sensed the presence of something frightful and was seemingly too terrified to give us away.

The captive Krol, meanwhile, gagged and tightly bound, his face shoved against the doorframe, began making panicky muffled noises.

'What'll I do with him, Chief? Shoulds I puts him out of his misery?' whispered Bran, putting his foot on the terrified priest's neck.

'I gave him my word we wouldn't kill him,' Tiroc Og replied. 'Take him back to the others. His dead fellows'll keep him warm – alive fer a whiles anyway – and he's more out the way there.'

Bran nodded and began to drag him away. Then Tiroc Og added, 'I've had a thought. Take off his robe – I'll swap it fer mine.'

The change was quickly made. When Bran returned, Tiroc Og whispered, 'Now, my friends, we're going into the nest of the devils. But, inside these robes, think Morok, think Ferok.'

'How do we do that?' I asked.

'Remember the ways they walk, how they disdain their lesser fellows. It'll need to convince. Keep yer hoods up; yer faces and yer weapons hidden.'

'And if we're challenged?' I glanced at Bran's huge frame, bigger than any Morok – and in an ill-fitting robe. He smiled and made a strangulation gesture – how he'd react if we were stopped.

'I've thought of this. Now, Bran. With yer hood up yeh could easily pass fer an Aguan. There are many Aguan bodygaurds in the service of Kahl and his priests. But if 'tis to work Bran, yeh must behave as a mute. I understand a little Morok and can utter a few grunts at least. My understanding is better than my speakin' though.

In this robe, only another Krol – or Ferok – would challenge me anyway. Anything trickier we'll have to deal with somehow.'

'I'll practice me non-speakin',' said Bran, laughing and putting a hairy finger to his lips.

'What's your plan, Tiroc Og?' I asked.

'Well, we needs find out these places where the prisoners are. So, we needs listen close whilst we're among the enemy, hope that one o' the devils 'ill give something useful away. Are yeh ready?'

'Never more,' said Bran, dropping three small pebbles by the doorframe. 'Lead on, Chief.'

We moved cautiously along the corridor in the direction of the Morok troop and came to a rusted iron door in a frame, the joists broken and sagging. Kahl's army, I'd learned, only ever built one kind of construction: palisades, lines of roughly hewn tree trunks lashed together with coir ropes and piled into the ground or thrown together as walls. Repairs to structures from earlier eras seemed to be beyond their capabilities. The door itself was twisted and ajar. From beyond came a babble; a multitude of voices, clanging and barking noises. The *Solon* quivered, but faintly – a signal of enemy presence, but perhaps not threat.

''Tis the courtyard,' Tiroc Og whispered as he cracked open the door a little wider. 'As yeh better understand their speaking, Osian, yeh must now lead, Bran next. I'll follow. Remember, keep to the sides, hoods over yer heads, mitts inside yer sleeves. Should anyone challenge yeh just point back at me – as yer superior.'

Once through the door we were on a covered timber walkway running round the sides of a courtyard open to the sky. Tiroc Og urged us to walk to the right, close to the tor wall and deep in the shadows, me between him and Bran. As we strode forward, I could make out on the far side of the courtyard part of a curving wall – the base of the other of Elvintal's fabled tors. The walkway rafters above us hung with fire smoke, deepening the shadows. The courtyard itself was jammed with canvas stalls displaying cooked food and cages packed with chickens and miserable-looking small pigs and goats. On some stalls were flagons of bubbling *aki*, arrays of a strange yellow grain and cut slabs of the dried meat I understood to be *petican*. Around woodfires overhung with smoking racks of *akra* – fermented saltwater weed – lounged gaggles of Morok troopers of both sexes and in a variety of shapes and sizes, many unarmed. Groups circled the traders or crouched around games of dice.

We passed a pair of Ferok sitting at a trestle table playing some variation of *skim*, ironically the game of the gods. Next to them were some heavily armed figures of a tribe I'd never seen before. Their faces were skeletal and marble-white, their eyes coal black, their chins pointed and their noses long. The hoods of their ice blue robes were down, revealing scarred bony heads and blood-red spiked necklaces round their necks. Taller than any Ferok, their visage was ferocious. I couldn't help but stare. The *Solon* trembled violently at my back as if urging me forward, away from these frightful looking creatures.

'Red Skraeling,' whispered Bran, following my gaze. 'Krachter's bodyguard. Dangerous as Okwa!' I shuddered as one of this legendary tribe glanced in my direction, sniffed the air, scowled, then turned away. The most notorious of the old tribes of Manau, rarely seen outside their arctic homelands – at least, not until the coming of the Morok. We were deep in the smoky shadows, and the Skraelings were a safe distance from us, yet I trembled along with the *Solon*, unaware I'd stopped moving until Bran nudged me forward through presses of Morok stinking of *petican* and *aki*. His burly frame attracted occasional glances from the courtyard crowd but no challenges. Mostly, the Morok jumped aside to make way for Tiroc Og in his high priest's robe – and Bran, his huge bodyguard.

The wall on the far side of the courtyard was overhung with balconies opening into dark spaces beyond. They were empty but one. On its rail perched a black hawk like bird with a purple hood over its eyes, a stripe of grey-white feathers to one side, and red and blue hunting tresses hanging from its talons. Krachter's eagle! I scanned the balcony to see if Kahl's lieutenant was there but could see no-one in its recess.

I was arrested by an appalling sight a little further along. A little stance from the eagle were a group of emaciated Barod, the gentlest of all the tribes, with iron rings around their necks and struggling under the weight of some huge wooden beams partly attached to a construction of some kind. A Ferok in chainmail was screaming at them. Another was lashing a whip. I trembled with rage. At home, Barod – Beaver tribe – were close clan friends: hard-working, gentle, loyal to those who employed them for their great skills in carpentry and construction. Here, they were slaves – and being abused! I tried to suppress my fury with deep breaths, promising myself there would be a reckoning.

The press thinned out, allowing us to walk briskly in single file under the eaves, the walkway now curving to the right. Further round we came to an opening, a passage going back inside the tor. The *Solon* had been quivering steadily throughout, but just as we reached the passage it sent a violent icy wave into my back. Suddenly a Ferok stepped out of the darkness, right in front of me, taking me by surprise. In a priestly robe. Krol!

Before I could react, he stopped in front of me and spoke in guttural Morok. 'Raige, brother. Is it yeh? Back from Clachoile? Were it successful – did yeh manage to fool thon Brach chief dog?'

I hesitated in my step, wondering what on earth to say or do. My heart beat hard as I tried to gather a response. But then the *Solon* began to thrum at my back. A cool blankness seemed to descend on me and I found myself calmly responding, my words coming out of my mouth in Morok: 'Yes, 'tis I. We mus' see Lord Krachter immediately. We've urgent news from Clachoile. I don't suppose yeh know where he is right now?' I could see Tiroc Og ahead of me, striding on unawares, and could feel Bran bristling at my back.

'Brother Raige, what be yer haste?' he replied, puffing up his chest and folding his hands into the sleeves of his robe. 'Yeh means the rebel plan to assault Rakhaus? Don't worry, he already knows, hah! 'Ave no fears. Rakhaus is stormproof. All our troops 'n ships are in place, ready and waitin' fer 'em.' With a grim cackle, he added, 'Lord Krachter 'ill unleash *haken* – warfare – like nothin' ever seen before. So, whatever yeh knows of their whereabouts yeh can tell me.'

'I cannot be gossipin' now with such as yeh,' I said. 'There's no time.'

'Pah, Raige,' he snapped. I had to tread carefully. Behind me I could feel Bran, hovering close. 'Yeh knows I'm one o' Krachter's inner council,' said the Krol, puffing up his chest. Then his eye caught Bran, hovering close. 'Anyways, who's thon – yer big friend? Not seen "im before.' Bran moved closer, towering over him. We couldn't risk being exposed, here in this crowded bosom of the enemy.

'Tis our Aguan bodyguard, 'ees new,' I said. 'Forget 'im. We're in a hurry. Delay us longer and I'll tell Krachter yeh held us back. Where is he?'

Whether because of my empty threat or Bran's bulk, the Krol bowed again then said, more formally, 'I am but my master's servant. Come, brother Raige. I can bring yeh straight to him. Come.' He turned away and beckoned, only then noticing Tiroc Og waiting in a recess. The Krol paused for a moment and bowed deeply to the shaman but kept going. The three of us fell in behind.

We padded openly along the walkway through a thick press of Morok troopers making way for us with deferential, even fearful, looks. Then leaving the courtyard, we began to climb a stairwell that spiralled upwards, but back into the Tor of Doors. Bran nudged me, whispering, 'What's happenin', Osian? Where we goin'?'

'Says he's taking us to Krachter,' I whispered back.

'I hopes yer knows what yer doin'.'

As we ascended, the Krol made conversation. 'Ye'll be 'ere in time for tonight's ceremony? We'd have a gossip then, surely? Can't wait to get yer news.'

'Of course, of course,' I said, the words tumbling from my mouth in gruff Morok. Then I asked, 'Tonight's ceremony. Remind me, I've been away. What be the occasion, like?'

'I suppose yeh didn't know, brother Raige? 'Tis the first o' 'em traitors to be hanged this moon – and on thon new contraption they're buildin' over there, yeh mu's 'ave seen it,' he replied, adding, 'Can't wait t' see 'em squeal.'

'Which traitors?' I could not stop myself asking, adding, 'There be so many.'

''Tis thon old boat keeper, Eronn. Gwior or Gwion or some such is the name in him.'

I heard a soft intake of breath from Bran, behind me.

'Yeh mean the old Fearsaig – the ferry keeper?'

'That's the one. They says there's another to go wi' im – an Albin dog, one of 'em ghost-faced smiths.'

My stomach lurched, a wave of fury shaking me from head to foot. I spluttered, 'Not by chance thon captured Albin with the Eronn dam?'

'Yes – and her with 'em witch's eyes. Make yeh creep, they do. Yes, yes.'

I faltered on the step. Mara. My poor mother, in the claws of these devils!

'What's up?' Tiroc Og whispered to me.

'Eh? What wiz that?' stuttered the Krol, turning and screwing his eyes into the darkness behind me.

I coughed and pointed to my throat. 'Scuse the dust in my throat. Ah him, tis jez my companion. Sharin' a joke, like.'

95

'Aye. 'Tis thirstmakin' work, travellin',' he responded, turning his back to me and resuming the ascent. 'Yeh'll be gettin' Krachter's best *aki* tonight I 'spects. Skraelandia's finest. I'm hoping to join yeh after we've brought the prisoners down.'

'Aye,' I spat out, feeling sick to my bones. 'I'll look forward to that. What… what did the prisoners do, that they're to be…' I gulped, '… hanged for?'

'In league with them rebels in Erainn. One of 'em was caught the other night talkin' to a harrier, tryin' to send a message. Didn't work, of course. Lord Krachter's eagle made short work o' thon infernal bird I hears. An' now the pair are to squeal their last breath. Can't wait fer it,' he chuckled.

One of Tiroc Og's faithful messenger tribe – slaughtered! I clenched my fist, fighting the urge to run this devil through with my sword.

'Krachter's laid a trap for thon sorceress Cana-Din and her band 'o scum – includin' thon wizard, Wildcat – what's 'ee called, mmm yes, Tiroc Ugh,' he continued with a cackle. 'Soon there'll be no more traitor chiefs left t' hang.'

I breathed deeply, remembering Grandfather's advice when emotions get out of control. But as we reached the top of the steps and entered a dark corridor, the Krol glanced back at us just as a strong draught of air flew down the passage. My hood was blown back. I yanked it quickly over my face. But Bran's hood had also blown back and he wasn't so quick. The Krol saw it. He stopped, squinted back at me and said, 'Raige, yer friend is very ugly. Does he speak ugly? I've not heard 'im.'

'He's a mute,' I answered. 'He doesn't speak. But he's good at killing traitors. Slowly, till they squeals.'

The Krol didn't answer, taking in Bran – now hooded again – from head to foot. But his brow knotted and his eyes darkened.

Shooting a glance at me, he hissed, turned away and quickened his pace. When he'd got a few lengths away, he broke into a run.

With three mighty leaps Bran was on him, huge mitt tight over the Krol's mouth, lifting him as if it was a bag of grain, then dropping him to the floor. Prostrate, I saw his neck twisted at an impossible angle. Dead.

Noises came from ahead. The *Solon* quivered violently. 'Quick,' whispered Tiroc Og, 'pick him up, Bran, carry him. Osian, be ready to explain that he's fallen, is hurt.'

A pair of Ferok, rings of keys jangling at their waists, rounded the corridor, babbling excitedly. Hood up, I strode forward, followed by Tiroc Og, then Bran, holding the dead Krol across his chest.

'Who goes? What's this?' said one, coming to a sudden stop. 'What's up with brother Kraike?'

We kept moving.

''Tis only I, Raige,' I grunted back in Morok. 'Move out t' way there. Can't you see he's fallen? I'm taking him fer medicine. Let the mute past. Hurry now. Move aside.'

'Steady on there, friend Raige. Let me see,' said one, brushing past me towards Bran. But he got no further. In the rapid flurry of movement that followed, both Ferok were on the ground, stone dead. Tiroc Og wiped his blade on their robes and said, 'I'll lift one, Osian, you drag the other. We must find a place to hide 'em. Go quickly.'

We ran along the corridor with our victims as best we could, passing doors to the right and left. From above came a low howling. 'Mastiffs,' muttered Tiroc Og, looking up, then peering at an open passage to the right. 'I'm hopin' from memory one of these leads up towards the brig over to the Tor o' Winds. Them rooms to the left – old cells of the holy ones. We can dump the bodies in there.'

Bran pushed at the doors, but all were locked. The howling from above became louder, more insistent, as if the dogs sensed our presence below. Then I remembered the big key with the Morok insignia. 'Try this,' I said, passing it to Bran. It worked immediately on the first door. A master key! Inside, the cell was empty, but there were signs of recent occupancy: an overturned flagon, a couple of empty plates, a filthy smell.

'Quick, get them in here,' Tiroc Og said. We dragged the bodies in, I re-locked the door and we carried on. But, passing the third door I picked up a familiar scent – a smell from home, from my young days, a fragrance of *patchli* flowers, the ones we were sent out to collect in our canoes on a rising moon – that Mara dried, pressed and with our help, extracted the oil she used as her own unique perfume all her life. It was the scent of my mother!

Heart racing, I pushed at the door. It was unlocked. Inside were signs of use: dishes, bowls and under a slit window, a worktable and hanging on the wall a fragment of a familiar cloth. Examining it I saw it was the fringe of an Eronn robe, torn from the collar. It was deep blue. Deep blue. Mara's colour.

I held it to my nose and breathed in the deep fragrance of water flower. Fresh as if it had just been worn. 'Mother's!' I exclaimed. My eyes were moist, my voice choking. 'She's just been here.' With trembling legs, I stumbled over to the worktable. On it was a tool rack, empty except for two small hammers: fine smithing tools, the ones she used for making jewellery. 'Her tools.' Something on the floor caught my eye. I stooped and picked out of the straw a half-finished brooch with intricate details. But as I felt its shape I recoiled and dropped it. Three talons. She'd been making totem icons for the Morok. Unbelievable –except of course she was a captive. Would have been made to do this. I wiped my eyes and looked over at my friend.

'We must keep moving,' Tiroc Og said. 'Courage, brother.'

'Someone's coming,' said Bran, who'd been standing watch at the door.

'Back inside,' Tiroc Og urged. 'Use thon key, Osian. Quickly, bolt it.'

From the corridor came the sound of voices, arguing. They stopped just outside. The door handle turned. We held our breaths, swords out and moved to the sides, standing ready beside the door. A key was inserted, turned, and re-turned. But nothing happened. They pushed at the door, and someone kicked it – in vain. Then came a long pause, with angry muttering from the corridor.

'I keep tellin yeh,' said one voice. 'Yer wastin' my time. Thon She-Eronn dog's already been taken.'

Another said, 'Try again. We needst check.'

Once more the key was turned and released. 'Cursed thing,' said the first. 'Where's thon Kraike? 'Ees got the master. And them guards with the other keys; where's em devils gone?'

'Probably drunk somewheres,' came the reply.

'Well, we haven't time – the trial be startin' soon,' barked the first voice. 'I don't want to miss seein' Krachter take their 'eads off.'

I stiffened; my jaw clenched.

The footsteps retreated and the voices faded. Tiroc Og unlocked the door and looked out. 'Gone. Let's go,' he whispered. 'What were they saying, Osian?'

As we left, I explained.

'This so-called trial must be imminent,' he responded. 'We needs gets up to where we can see what's going on and… int…' The word died in his breath. it was "intervene," I was sure. If he didn't, I certainly would. Even if it were my own death.

My blood boiling, we followed the Morok down the corridor and arrived at another set of three doors. The first two were locked, but the third easily opened into a stairwell. 'If they didn't have the right key, they must have gone this way,' he said. Bran placed three tiny pebbles on the corner of the threshold and we went through, ascending a set of steps spiralling round a wall, bows now outside our robes, ready armed.

At the next landing, Tiroc Og said, 'I'm remembering now,' and pointed to a tiny open annex on one side with carvings of prayer flags around the entrance. 'That's the flag room. The holy ones used it to store the prayer cloths they flew from the top of the tor.' Then he stopped, his head cocked. Further up the corridor beyond the annex, red light was trickling through an opening. He took a hesitant step towards it, then held up a hand. 'Wait,' he said, ducking to all fours, gesturing us to stay low and follow him.

The opening led onto a balcony, where a babble of noise came up from below. At my back the *Solon* was quivering – danger, near. We crouched below the stone ledge.

'Something's going on,' he whispered, 'Osian, what can yeh hear?'

I put my ear to the stone. Despite being too far away to hear speech above the babble of the courtyard beyond, I could clearly hear a deep voice barking instructions in Morok: ''Ave 'em brought down to the waiting chamber. The blue-eyed dam can look down on her old dog being tried fer treason, then watch 'im dying with the Fearsaig at the stroke o' mid-sun. She'll 'ave her turn at the next moon – 'less Kahl has another use fer her,' he added with a cackle.

Blue-eyed dam? Mara! It was just as that Krol had said: my father was to die with Gwion-Din – and she after. My chest heaved with rage. I stood up, hand on my sword hilt, and looked over the ledge. Three robed figures were standing on the edge of the courtyard, their backs to me. One was walking away; two others remained standing below the balcony. The tallest of the two wore a white robe with short sleeves, revealing blue-brown chain mail on his arms. On one shoulder was the black eagle from before, hood off, its head twisting round. Krachter! The *Solon* shivered violently at my back.

The other figure, in a blood-red robe, was much broader than any Ferok I'd seen. On the hood was the mark of the Morok inside a black circle. Poking out from a sleeve I saw a furred, clawed hand like Tiroc Og's. Wildcat tribe. What!

My hands were itching on my crossbow, struggling with the overwhelming temptation to slaughter the pair on the spot. I must have shown it, for Tiroc Og grabbed my shoulders and dragged me back below the ledge. 'Careful, yeh'll be seen. Yeh'll get yer chance – not now.'

Below, the deep voice was speaking. 'Kahl's given the signal fer the trial to commence.'

'Aye, Lord Krachter,' said the other, a voice like Tiroc Og's, but the tone was cruel, sinister. 'The prisoners are below, in my waitin' chamber, ready to be brought out and fer my *gallowglass* to take 'em in its arms,' he said with a cackle.

It was too much. My head was swimming; hatred flooded my body. I started up again. 'Down,' hissed Bran, hauling me back. I felt a warmth in my lower back. The *Solon* was still quivering, but gently. It too was trying to calm me. The sensation cooled the urgent frenzy of fury that had been coursing through my body. I was able to gather myself and explain what I'd heard, my voice breaking, adding, 'I could've put a bolt in Krachter's back just then.'

'That would have achieved little,' whispered Tiroc Og. 'They'd have killed us all before we got anywhere near yer kin. One of 'ems Krachter, yeh say. Describe what yeh see.'

'Like the jay Ferok I saw at the ruins of Iteron. Blue-brown mail, a white robe. Patch over one eye. Black eagle on his wrist.'

'That's him certainly. And the other?'

'Broad – not Ferok – at least I don't think. Long red robe, hooded. Didn't see the face, but…' I hesitated. 'I saw his hand – like yours. Wildcat.'

'Yahl save us. That's Morc!' Bran spluttered. 'Kahl's executioner, cold-blooded varmint.' He pushed a clenched fist against the wall and spat. 'Wildcat, to be sure, to his shame, an escaped murderer, a traitor to the free tribes – to his fathers.'

Tiroc Og put a hand on both our shoulders, saying quietly, 'Calm, brothers.'

'How do we get to this waiting chamber?' I whispered, still shaking with fury, urgent to act, to do something, anything!

'It'll likely be at courtyard level,' he replied. 'To get there we needs go back and down.'

Suddenly, from behind came the sound of running feet on the stone steps and a clashing of mail and steel. 'Quick, follow me,' urged Tiroc Og.

We left the balcony, still crouching, then stood and ran along the corridor and round the bend till we reached another stairwell. There we were met again by the sound of tramping feet and clashing metal coming up the stairs. Both ways down and back were blocked.

The eagle, of course; it had been the eagle. When it twisted its head around, I'd glimpsed its eyes. As a hunter, I should have known. If I'd seen my prey's eyes, then my prey had seen me.

And now we were trapped.

7

THE TRIAL

A bruptly, the commotion below halted. Tiroc Og sniffed the air, shook his head and whispered, 'The varmits have stopped – but 're still there – can smell their stink. Maybes like foxes in a fog they don't know how many of us there are – or even what we are. I can smell their fear.'

But they were still coming along the corridor behind, slowly, gingerly. Here were no wild woods or rocks for us to merge into, just endless doors, stairs and corridors all leading straight into the heart of the enemy – the bowels of their stolen lair.

Bran glanced back down the corridor and stood to his full height, taking in huge breaths, his great frame expanding, resolving, no doubt, to kill as many Morok as he could before the end. For a warrior it was the only way to leave life, to go down fighting.

'The firelogs?' I ventured to Tiroc Og, remembering the incredible weapon.

'Can't use 'em where we are, Osian,' he said, resignation in his voice. 'It'd close up our ways out – even bring these old stones down on our heads.'

There was still no movement from below. Why had they stopped? What were they waiting for? For their fellows on the corridor to attack first?

Tirog Og, rarely lost for a plan, sniffed the air and shrugged, looking more puzzled than fearful. For once, it seemed, the great hunter-shaman was struggling.

'Grandfather always told me,' I whispered, 'that when cornered, in a fight or a game of *skim*, try to do what your opponent would expect the least.'

'Yes, Osian, but here – what would that be?'

'Well, as you said, they probably don't know who or what we are – yet. Or how we are disguised.' Krachter's eagle had seen a fleeting glimpse of a hooded figure in deep shadow. Something it didn't like. But what, or who?

'What d'ye have in mind?'

I explained my idea. He smiled and nodded. 'We've nothing to lose. Our lives if we stay here. Our lives if we go, but maybe thon way there's a chance… what d'yeh think, Bran?'

The Brach smiled broadly. 'Let's do it.'

'Then, ready yer weapons,' said Tiroc Og. 'Yahl be with us.'

So, with our hoods up, our weapons bared beneath our robes, I led the way down the stairwell, at first muttering chanting sounds. Then, through the quivers of the *Solon*, new phrases began forming in my mouth and I chanted in horrid tones: 'Kahl be with us; Kahl save us; we are Morok.'

At the bottom of the stairs five troopers stood before us, spears and axes at the ready. I breathed out: only five! They looked hesitant, unsure. No mastiffs. Tirog Og, behind me, joined in my chanting – a series of grunts. The troopers, staring curiously, shuffled awkwardly but made no move. As we neared, I felt the shivering of the *Solon* growing stronger and my voice with it.

In brusque tones, I said, 'What's with the fuss, scum dogs? Get out 'o the road. How dare yeh stand in our way!'

The lead trooper, looking confused, began to jabber something. I carried on chanting. The *Solon's* shivering rose to a frenzy until the air around me seemed to hum and quiver. Then, as before, time seemed to slow, slower than the movement of the tides or the moon in the night sky. A knife flew past my ear. The lead trooper dropped to the ground. Another knife from behind felled the second, my sling-stone embedded in the forehead of a third. A crossbolt from Bran dropped a fourth. The one left standing, eyes agape, opened his mouth to call out, but fell soundlessly to the ground, my grandfather's sword in his chest.

Real time returned to reveal the carnage at our feet. I stood for a moment, half in horror, half in astonishment at the speed with which we'd acted, until Bran pushed me aside and ducked to retrieve his knife and crossbolt. 'That cell over there,' urged Tiroc Og, 'quickly, put 'em in there.' It was open. Dragging them inside we locked the door and continued the direction we'd taken before at this lower level. The *Solon* was sentient; no-one seemed to be following us now.

Maybe, I pondered, the encounter with the guards was not as I'd seen it. Old Annan's advice – with the help of the *Solon* – had got us through, as if two forces older than I were working together, as if someone – or something – was watching over us. So far. Or we were just lucky? Swift of hand, eye and foot though we seemed to be, such luck as this couldn't possibly last.

Gaps in the walls we were passing revealed the courtyard below, the space brimming with noise, smoke and smells, but there was a new feel to it: a buzz of excitement; the quick rattle of voices anticipating something about to happen; a sinister unhealthy air of expectation.

'How many smoke sticks d'yeh have, Bran?' asked Tiroc Og, stopping as we reached a long curving bend in the corridor.

'Six, Chief.'

'Yeh know what to do – what we talked about before? And how timing is everything.'

'I do.'

Tiroc Og pointed to the end of the corridor. 'Yeh two must wait here for the moment. Beyond thon corner is the low-level brig crossin' the moat 'tween the two tors. Look fer me down below. If yeh see me, wait for my signal, then make for the brig. I'll follow yeh. Don't wait for me,' he instructed.

'Where are you going?' I asked, caught by surprise. I'd not been included in whatever plan he'd made with Bran. Tiroc Og was going down there? Into that nest of vipers, without us?

'Ye'll see. Do whatever Bran says. Stick together like the water willows, both of yeh. I'll join yeh soon as the great Yahl allows.' He darted into a narrow stairwell and disappeared. I stared after him, trembling in my stomach. I'd become so used to his watchful wise presence, more of a father than a brother; without him I'm sure, I'd be long dead.

'Leave 'im, Osian,' said Bran, sensing my discomfort. 'He knows what he's doin' – allis.'

'But...'

'Come, brother, come. We'll wait back here,' he said, indicating a recess in the inner wall where the old stone structure had collapsed. The corridor was very narrow at this point and, standing on a rubble pile, we were able to see through a gap on the outside wall down into the courtyard. Deep in the shadows, we were unseen by the milling crowd below; free to observe the proceedings.

Looking down I saw the wooden contraption those sad enslaved Barod had been building, now wheeled into a new position, right under the balcony on the far side where we'd first seen Krachter's eagle.

'Is that the… the *gallowglass*?' My voice shook as I remembered the conversation between Krachter and the Wildcat in the red robe.

'Aye. 'Tis an execution machine, Red Skraeling invention.' Bran answered, a chill in his voice. He put a warning hand on my wrist. 'Don't let yer rage overcome yeh.' The *Solon* quivered and I tried to calm myself.

Then a bell rang: once, twice, three times. Solemn, drawn-out tones that echoed round the courtyard like the sky hammers of Yahl. A doom bell. My stomach trembled.

Figures began to appear on the balcony above the machine: two Krol, followed by Krachter, the great black eagle, now hooded, tethered to his wrist. Kahl's wicked lieutenant grasped the balcony rail, surveyed the crowd nodded approvingly at the *gallowglass*, smiled grimly and stroked the bird's head. 'Bring out the traitor dogs,' he commanded.

A metal grille opened below the balcony. A stunted, hollow-eyed Ferok came out, keys dangling about his waist. He pulled a figure in chains – a tall Eronn in torn robes, thin-faced, aged grey mane, no longer tricoloured and flecked with red dust. But his head was held aloft, his bearing proud. The crowd gasped as if moved by the sight of this noble figure.

My fists clenched. My eyes filled with tears. Beside me Bran uttered a low growl.

This must surely be Gwion-Din the elder, the ferry keeper, my grandfather's friend. My heart lurched as I watched him turning to look across the crowd, seemingly unmoved by anything he saw. There was no hatred in that look. If anything, he looked on them with pity. His eyes were radiant blue, the colour of my mother's, but the hue deeper: penetrating, fathomless, more like the eyes of Erin's, the vision in the Marten's fire. At my back the *Solon* trembled and pulsed, the movement coming in waves, like the heaving of deep sobbing.

In all my young years I'd never seen another being with such a graceful bearing. Little surprise Grandfather had thought so highly of him and wanted us to meet, wanted him to be the first guide on my journey into Erainn. I found it hard to believe he was just a ferry keeper, surely a profession demeaning to such as he. I thought that if there had indeed been kings, as in the Manu fables, or in the sculptured images in the ancient stone scrolls I'd seen in my schooling, this would surely be one, a chief above all chiefs.

The jailor pulled roughly on another chain. A slender bowed figure in a torn stained blue robe came forward. My heart felt as though it would burst from my chest. Faron. My father!

At the sight of him, the crowd began to roar, screaming "traitor, traitor dog". I clutched at my crossbow, every muscle in my body twitching to act.

'Don't.' Bran grabbed my shoulder. 'We wait.'

I knew I could put a bolt between Krachter's eyes from where I stood. But I stiffened and bit my lip.

Krachter raised his arm in some kind of salute. A great hush descended on the courtyard. I followed their gaze to a high balcony projecting from the side of a colossal circular structure rising beyond the passage Tiroc Og had pointed out – the Tor of the Winds. Against the railings stood a single figure, behind a pair of Red Skraeling. It was my mother! Mara.

Feeling dizzy with the effort to stop myself calling out, I clutched at Bran's arm to stop from falling over. Mara's glorious mane was covered in a hood, with tips of white showing under the rim. Her chin – all I could see of her face – was wet with grief. Behind her, the Red Skraeling slipped back and a figure in a white robe hovered briefly in the shadows, then was gone. Mara was looking down, faltering as if about to faint. One of the Skraeling darted forward, grabbed her and held her up against the railing.

My heart pummelled wildly; tears raced down my cheeks. My hands on my crossbow so tight I felt it could snap.

'We wait, we wait,' murmured Bran, his hand on my shoulder. 'We do nothing. 'Tis not our moment.' Then he whispered, 'Look,' and pointed to a gate at one end of the courtyard through which poured scores of troopers, this time tall Ferok, heavily armed, dressed for battle.

They positioned themselves in the centre of the courtyard, roughly pushing back the existing crowd, knocking over some of the stalls, sending the stallholders and their wares flying. They even turned on any who were slow to get out the way, clubbing them to the ground. Cruel even to their own kind! The crowd scurried further back, out of the way.

'Where is Tiroc Og?' I hissed.

'Jes' wait, Osian, wait and watch,' he replied. I shook with frustration, yet I had to stay calm, had to trust my friends.

Krachter beamed at the new arrivals, ignoring the mayhem they'd caused, then addressed the crowd. 'All yeh of the Great Morok Way. We're here to do justice. Here before yeh are the very worst 'o those who'd betray our great cause, do harm to our beloved leader, Kahl our saviour. He has commanded that here, before all gathered on this day, the traitors standin' afore yeh must speak fer theyselves, do account for their actions, afore receiving the justice of the Morok, the will of the Great One.'

This was welcomed by cheers and whistles and a slow, deathly chant of 'Morok, Morok, Morok,' coming from the Ferok troops. So, this was a trial? A final humiliation of Gwion-Din, before his and my father's cold-blooded murder – and a dagger in the heart of Mara, forced to see her loving mate suffer and die.

Bran kept his hand heavy on my shoulder as waves of anxiety washed over me. Where was Tiroc Og? When were we going to do something? Anything? Gwion-Din's guards whipped him round on his chains to face his tormentor. 'Great Gwion-Din the Fearsaig,' said Krachter in Ironese, in a mocking tone. Then, as he waited for an underling to translate into Morok for the crowd: 'Yeh've acted treasonous to the lawful authority of Erainn. Yeh're here present with yer fellow traitor, the outlander Faron, sire to the thief Osian, one of the cowardly rebels who've murdered our brothers and are sworn to destroy us. Yeh were seen trying to contact them – no doubt to get them rescue you. Well,' he laughed. 'Look about, O proud Eronn. D'yeh see them here? Have they come here to save yer sorry soul?'

'No!' yelled the crowd, following the translation. My stomach heaved; I wanted to cry out that I was here, and that I'd send Krachter to his death. I didn't care that I'd been named. I wanted him to see my face, know who I was when I took the life from him, dispatch him to the hell reserved for quislings and murderers.

'Ye'll die together,' Krachter continued. 'For yer sins yeh'll dangle from the *gallowglass*, just as these have done before ye.'

Reaching down, he raised up a pole bearing the feathery corpses of a pair of harriers, Tiroc Og's messengers, broken at the neck, their once proud feather manes hanging limp. The crowd cheered, howled and bayed. I felt Bran stir angrily beside me. But if they were indeed Tiroc Og's, one bird was out there still. Had it got through? Was hope alive yet?

Krachter spoke on, his voice rising and falling. 'On yeh, proud Gwion-Din, there is crime yet greater. Kahl's high priests came to yeh fer a safe crossing; put their trust in yeh. Instead yeh took 'em to their doom; drowned 'em like rats.' His voice raised to a crescendo as he said, 'Murdered! Well, old Gwion-Din the Fearsaig, yer dark night has come.'

The crowd roared; the troops chanted. Krachter dropped the birds and raised his hand for silence.

'Speak, old water dog. What d'yeh have to say of yer guilt?'

After a pause, Gwion-Din spoke in tones solemn and proud. 'You talk of murder. You, Krachter, dogsbody to the outlander who has persecuted the rightful guardians of once fair Erainn, the holy land of the gods, destroyed our homes and habitats, enslaved us to make weapons of war, starved our offspring, and poisoned the very earth. You,' he said, raising his voice, cracked and broken yet still audible above the jeering crowd, his words somehow sailing above them, 'who incur the wrath of the gods. You, I tell you, *your* night will come.'

Someone shouted aloud a translation for the benefit of the Morok assembly. These were not the words they heard. Instead, the crowd were fed a series of curses and insults. At this, they erupted in a yowl of scorn and fury.

Krachter merely smiled. 'Hah. Wrath, what wrath? It is yeh who are deserving of their wrath. Do yeh deny that, with this Albin here, yeh conspired with the outlaw Cana-Din and the renegade Tiroc Og, to attack us here in our home, to kill us and our valiant followers – murder us all as we slept?'

More jeering and whistling. Gwion-Din, head high, didn't respond.

Krachter, picking up and brandishing up the dead birds, pressed for a response. 'Yeh and thon Albin dog were seen talking to these messengers of the renegades, by Xanon here–' at which the eagle at his wrist squawked – 'and here in holy Rakhaus itself, 'afore she killed 'em. D'yeh deny this?'

Gwion-Din spoke out as if in a trance. 'Who am I to deny what your creature may tell you? It is true these harriers came to the window of the cell where I have been imprisoned. I asked them only tidings of my kin. I have no need of rescue – no-one should be at risk for the sake of my failing body. If you hadn't killed them, they would have passed on my message, for they are creatures of truth. And the Albin is also innocent of your charge. When the harriers came, Faron asked only of his cub, his own father, his home. He wished not to risk the life of Mara. You are misguided. Kill me if you wish. But spare him. Spare her.'

None of this was translated. A tense expectant silence fell upon the crowd.

Krachter looked irritated, maybe stung by Gwion-Din's bravery and the calmness with which he spoke. 'Do yeh then deny the charge of murdering the holy priests of Kahl?' he barked.

Gwion-Din stared at his accuser. 'In truth, two of Kahl's Krol came to me the night of the great helm. The river was in the sky. Unpassable. The ferry was tied down. They demanded passage at the point of a sword, did not heed my warnings, so desperate was their haste. Indeed, I saw that they were already ailing, almost to the death.'

'Yeh lie,' Krachter shouted. But there was something odd in his defiance, as if he knew this much. I remembered Tiroc Og telling me how deadly dangerous was the touch of the *Solon*, if unsheathed. And I'd seen the Krol that had taken it to be sealed by the beast in the cavern. Seen it being changed from something shiny to the dull shell I had in my *papose*. Their mission was their inevitable doom.

'There is more,' continued Gwion-Din. 'They carried with them a strange thing shielded in black – I know not what it was. Some of the black was on their faces and robes – evil-smelling stuff. Mid-water the storm threw us over, broke the boat into pieces. I don't know how I survived. All I remember is clutching on to the thing they carried. For it floated above the waves. Next thing I knew it was day and I was lying on the shore like so much flotsam, bits of the ferry lying around me. I never saw the thing again – nor your Krol. All was swept away.'

At my back, the *Solon* gave a pulse, as though recognising itself in the tale.

'Pah,' retorted Krachter, his eagle shaking its tresses. 'Yeh lie. Xanon saw ye rise from the river, unharmed, smiling. Yeh *stole* that which saved yeh and left it where it would be found by another – he whom yeh were meant to meet – the young dog of thon Albin here. Now, what do yeh say to that?'

It was strange to hear myself spoken of as though I was a knowing participant in some great plan, when all that had happened to me was just a series of accidents. But I knew now at least the circumstances by which the *Solon* had been removed from the cavern to the river where I had found it.

Gwion-Din didn't respond.

'Speak of yer guilt, old Fearsaig,' screamed Krachter. 'These are yer last words in this earth, make it a truth to yer gods afore yeh're taken to the *gallowglass* – and to eternal doom.'

The crowd had meanwhile maintained a steady chant which now erupted to a frenzied scream, rising up and up. 'Kill him, kill the water dog. Kill him!'

But the Eronn elder calmly lifted his head, stared Krachter in the eye and said, 'May Yahl forgive you for all that you have done. I'm ready to meet my fate; to go to a place beyond yer reach, to go the *sidhe*. However you choose to end my life is no matter. If I am guilty of anything it is of living too long to see the evil you have done to my tribe, my land. But I plead you, let the Albin smith and the She-Eronn go free. They have done nothing.'

Kahl's lieutenant took in a sharp breath, his hands clutching the railing so tightly I thought the metal would bend. 'They are of an accursed line – like yeh. We, Kahl, the tribes no longer have use fer them. They too must die. Enough of this. Morc!' he screamed.

A ripple of excitement ran through the crowd as the creature in the blood red robe and black hood walked into the space below the balcony. A hush fell upon the courtyard as he bowed to Krachter, then towards the crowd and the prisoners before glancing up to where Mara was being held.

Then, to my horror, he turned and looked towards where we stood as if he could see us in the shadows. He made a tiny gesture – a finger run over his throat, then threw his arms in the air. As one, the crowd turned their heads in our direction.

8

THE BELL TOR

All had dropped to their knees – all except my father and Gwion-Din, defiantly facing away. It was not us the crowd were staring at, but above our heads. I followed their gaze and saw a long violet sleeve stretch over the balcony edge.

At this the *Solon* quivered so violently I was almost knocked off my feet. From the sleeve emerged a clenched, shaking fist, opening gradually to reveal three misshapen fingers – talons like the claws of a vulture, pointing directly down at Gwion-Din. The hallmark of the Morok. Directly above us was the architect of all the misery that was being visited upon Erainn, the free tribes, and my family. Kahl the Skryer!

The sleeve was withdrawn. The doom bell struck again: once, twice, three times. Across the way Krachter turned to Morc, the figure in the blood-red robe, made a gesture, then lifting the eagle's hood he released it. It flew in our direction, but up towards Kahl, no doubt to be with him in this cruel moment of glory, the death of Kahl's "foes", and hovered in front of the balcony.

My mind raced. My body urged me to react. Kill someone, but who and how? Oddly, the *Solon* was quivering gently, the sensation was calming. *Not now*, I was being told, *not yet*. Then Morc made a tiny gesture which surprised me – it was the salute I'd seen the rebels using to each other when arriving or departing, a touch of two fingers on the forehead right above the eyes, then an uncurling palm, open and pointing slightly down. And in that moment, I saw something oddly familiar in the bearing of the one called Morc. Surely not... I stared in disbelief.

Bran whispered in my ear, 'Aye. It's Tiroc Og.'

'So, where's Morc?' But I'd already guessed the answer.

'Shhh, be ready to move, young 'un, stay close,' hissed Bran, whipping out his flint and sparking a firestick of a type I'd not seen before, squat and bulging at one end. The hovering bird saw the movement, suddenly dropped its head and let out an almighty shriek.

We'd been seen!

At this, 'Morc' raised his arm, Tiroc Og's green stone sparkling at the wrist. And Bran sprang into action, throwing the firestick into the crowd, then sparking and throwing another. They exploded with a colossal bang. Thick green smoke billowed everywhere, enveloping the crowd below. They began to panic, running in all directions, coughing and choking, looking for a way out.

'Put this o'er yer mouth, Osian,' urged Bran. 'Tie it at the back. 'Tis just smoke, not gas,' he said, handing me a damp bandana and tying another round his face. 'Ready now, take up yer sword and follow.'

We raced down the corridor then down some stairs and across the courtyard, scattering all in our way, darting wildly through a confusion of bodies, limbs and contorted, choking faces. I hardly knew which direction we were going in, but kept at Bran's heels, as close as I could.

But by the time we got to the other side, the prisoners – and Tiroc Og – had gone. Krachter's balcony was empty. Bran turned and threw another smoke stick into the panicking mob. My eyes streaming, I looked back across the courtyard up to the balcony where I'd seen the curved claw. And there he was, Kahl: a tall, hooded figure in a white robe with purple sleeves, the face wracked by turmoil – the expression almost a kind of sadness; the eyes white, glazed over – the colourless gaze of the unseeing. Kahl was blind!

His mouth was contorted with fury and hatred. I saw him stretch his arm directly towards me, raise and uncurl his talons. I felt a sudden pain in my chest, as if a claw had entered my body and was groping towards my back. I felt the *Solon* lurch. I dropped to the ground in agony, but somehow managed to stagger back up, lift and aim my crossbow. But he'd already gone. The balcony was empty.

'Come, Osian!' shouted Bran pointing to the dark passage Tiroc Og had indicated earlier, just visible in the grey swirling smoke. Moaning bodies littered the ground, crushed and trampled by the stampede, but as we picked our way around and over them, I heard a sudden blast of horns and howling mastiffs. Through a gate at the west end of the courtyard poured a mass of troopers, faces covered, and smashed through the mass of coughing, reeling flesh – directly towards us!

Running on, I glanced a group of armed masked figures in ill-fitting Ferok robes racing in single file along the walkway under Kahl's balcony. The sight almost stopped me in my tracks. The lead figure had the unmistakeable shape of an Eronn and poking out from the edge of his robe, Lakon's tell-tale bow! Among the others I saw a slender figure under whose hood protruded a truss of bright red hair. Gimin! Our friends were here. It was astonishing. We were not alone.

Then the figures were gone, lost in the side passages, the shadows and the smoke. And Bran was screaming, 'Hurry up! What yeh doin?'

117

I caught up with him as we left the courtyard. 'Bran,' I said, 'I'm sure I saw some of the others back there. Lakon... Gimin...'

'Don't count on it,' he said, falling behind me. 'Could well be a trick of the smoke – seeing faces we want to see. C'mon, keep going.'

Illusion or not, it had cheered me. Images of our friends, of Gimin, filled my head as we entered the opening that hugged the side of the tor, pushing aside the reeling Morok mob crouching below the layer of smoke. As we ran through, a shower of bolts clattered off the walls around us.

'Go ahead!' yelled Bran, one of his slender sticks in one hand, a flint in the other. 'I'll catch up.' Before I could argue, a huge explosion rocked the courtyard. Rubble, armour and blood flew everywhere. The force of it knocked me to my knees, debris splattering the ground around me, but I managed to crawl into the safety of the passage. Bran had used an explosive firestick.

A second blast sent a cloud of smoke and grit tearing up the passage. I glanced back anxiously. Bran? Where was he? Where were our friends in this mayhem?

To my relief, Bran re-appeared out of the fog, teeth gleaming white through the dust caking his face. 'Keep goin!' he shouted. We raced along the passage and up three sets of stairs past cowering, scuttling Morok. In this blinding chaos we were the least of their concerns.

The passage opened on to a tiny courtyard. Here was a most extraordinary construction: a gushing fountain of water pouring from high like a waterfall into a channel that curved around the wall of the second tor. Water slopped and dripped over the sides of the channel. High above, between the buildings hung a brig of rope and planks. A figure in a ragged stained Albin robe was being dragged on a chain along the brig. I glimpsed the face.

'Father!' I screamed.

Faron reacted. He grabbed hold of a cable. I crouched, loaded my crossbow and unleashed a bolt at the Morok, pulling him and scoring a direct hit. The devil crumpled to the swaying planks, the whip tumbling from his hands.

Racing forward, we mounted the steps up to the brig. Faron, tied to his captor, was slipping on the brig, trying to rise. I threw back my hood and shouted that we were coming. Grappling at the cable he lifted, he stared down at me in disbelief and mouthed my name.

Suddenly, two Ferok appeared on the far side of the brig and started loading crossbows. I fired a bolt – it flew into the face of the nearest, while his own shot whistled past my ear. The other one fell forwards into the moat, a bolt in his chest. Meanwhile, the body of the jailor was slipping off the brig, Faron with him. He was clutching at the cable; his face twisted with the strain. 'Father!' I screamed and reached to grab him. But too late, he was already tumbling towards the water. 'No!' I yelled. 'No!'

I made to dive in after him, but Bran held me back. 'Look, Osian, look!' he screamed, as I struggled against him, shouting 'Let me go!' Then I saw Faron's fall had been halted. He'd been pinioned against the stonework and was dangling like a puppet. A feathered arrow – Tiroc Og's colours – had hammered through a link in the chain and secured it to the wall below the brig.

'We'll be there, Father. We'll get you!' I cried.

As I clambered with Bran onto the swinging brig, I glimpsed a shadow perched on a ledge high above us, winds whipping at a blood-red robe and glimpsed Tiroc Og raising a conch to his face. Its call echoed through the air, bouncing around the walls.

We were able to reach the chain holding my father and pull him onto the structure. I knelt down and took him in my arms. Bran sliced through the chain at his wrists with his small axe. But Faron was motionless. Barely breathing.

'Father,' I moaned, fearing the worst. Wrapping my robe around him, I furiously rubbed his bleeding hands and bare feet. 'Don't die,' I whispered in his ear, tears running down my cheeks.

'Look, young 'un,' said Bran, pointing to his chest. It was moving – just. Pushing me aside, he hoisted my father to his shoulder. 'Yeh folks can cosy up later. We have work yet. Come.'

Once we were on the far side, Bran axed the cables connecting the brig to the stonework. With a loud snap it burst from its moorings and fell towards the moat below, ropes lashing the air. 'That'll hold 'em back. Let's hope Tiroc Og knows his way out o' this hellhole.' We raced along a corridor, but already Morok troopers had arrived at the other side and were arming crossbolts. We were in deadly range, but the smoke billowing up from below obscured us. I heard the odd bolt crashing around us – lost in the fog.

I pointed upwards and said to Bran, 'Mara, my mother, was on a balcony up there somewhere.'

'We needs join Tiroc Og 'afore we go looking anywheres else,' he replied sharply.

Behind us the smoke had turned to flames that were licking up the walls of the stonework. I thought of our friends and hoped that they were elsewhere and safe. I pointed the flames out to Bran. 'No way out for us back there anyways,' he muttered with a cursory glance backwards as we sped down the corridor. 'Jes' keeps goin',' he added. 'I'm hoping the gods stay with us. They have so far, anyways.'

As we ran, I saw Faron stirring on Bran's shoulder. He lifted his head, looked at me and gasped. 'Osian... Mara – save her, save her.'

'Stop, Bran,' I urged. 'Faron's awake.' I looked frantically around. 'There's a recess in the wall there. Put him down. I need to talk to him.' Bran halted laid him down gently and held his head and shoulders while I put my flask to Faron's lips: 'Drink, Father. It'll help.'

He lifted a hand to stroke my face. There were tears in his eyes – mine, too. 'My son. You've come. Annan sent you? He is well?'

I nodded. But so many moons had passed since I'd left home; there was no way of knowing. When I left, old Annan had been preparing for the next life. I could only hope he'd hold on to what remained of his time. But there were limits – even for an old warrior.

'You're different, son. Something's changed.'

'I'm older, father. I've become a fighter...'

'A warrior... as Annan wanted?' He looked up at Bran, taking in the ferocious face of my companion.

'Yes.'

'Warrior... of course,' he muttered. Long ago, Father had never taken the hunter's way; never had the warrior training. My grandmother, when she was alive, for some reason forbade it. Probably heard too many of Grandfather's wild stories. She used to say he'd made them up, always with a smile on her face, but never wanted Faron to take after him. And Faron had chosen Mara for a mate, an Eronn, the chosen tribe, peace-loving people by choice. What would they think of the ruthless killer I'd become?

'You were always Annan's apprentice. We knew you'd become like him...' He paused, his voice breaking. 'You wouldn't have got this far... otherwise.' He looked away, eyes glistening with tears. 'It was always so – in our line.'

'What do you mean?'

But he was struggling, his voice weak, leaving me wondering. Then he gasped, 'Something in you has changed. I see it in your eyes. There's a darkness... Osian...' Alarm seemed to flit across his countenance. Then his eyes closed, and his body sank into my arms.

Fresh tears ran down my face. 'Father, hold on. We need to find Tiroc Og; he will look to your injuries... help you.'

He half-opened his eyes. 'Tiroc Og. Cub of Annan's old friend? He's with you?' and took a deep, rattling breath. 'That gives me comfort. And who is this – your warrior companion?' He smiled weakly up at Bran.

'Bran is the name in him,' I said. 'He saved my life – more than once.'

'A good friend to have, Osian, a good friend. And Tiroc Og, where is he?'

'Looking for Gwion-Din – ahead somewhere.'

Bran was sniffing the air. 'Smoke,' he said. 'Nearby. The fire... coming this way. We needs move.'

The conflagration was following us. I could feel its heat in the stones beneath our feet. But there was no warning from the *Solon*. Fire. Was this a danger it did not recognise?

'They took brave Gwion-Din to Krachter,' Faron gasped. 'I heard the order. They took my Mara... before – I've not seen her for many a day – til now, on thon balcony.'

'I saw her too,' I said, my grip on my sword hilt tightening. 'We'll find her, we will.' But there was desperation in my voice. I feared for her, surrounded by menacing Red Skraeling. Why were the Morok doing all this? What was their interest in her? I couldn't imagine anyone – no matter how cruel – harming or wanting to harm such a gentle creature.

'Father, d'you know how we get up there?'

'She'll be on the Glassin level. Krachter's floor. Near the top of the Tor of the Winds. 'Tis in the sky. There are stairs... so many stairs,' he replied, coughing, every word an effort.

'Can we get up there from here?' Bran urged.

Faron glanced around. Then, eyeing the timbers above us, he gasped, 'No, not from here. This is only the Bell Tor. You'll needs be further over – easterly. Find the stairs and go all the way down, then back outside, further easterly round this Tor. 'Tis the next building over.'

I jumped up. 'We've taken a wrong turn.' The Bell Tor. I didn't remember Tiroc Og talking of this. Maybe he'd forgotten.

Bran didn't seem to know of it either. 'Another cursed building...' he grunted.

'Find her, before...' muttered Faron, drifting into unconsciousness.

Bran hoisted him onto his shoulders and we raced on, the wall of heat getting closer behind. There was smoke everywhere. Flames were darting like devils between the rafters above us; the beams were bursting alight like so much tinder. Why was the *Solon* so quiescent, just when I needed its help the most? Maybe against Morok it could intervene, but not a threat like this. Did it not sense fire?

We ran forward along the corridor, hoping almost beyond hope, smoke and flames following. What to do? Where was Tiroc Og? We had to find a way out of here – and to the high tor. Who could help us? I was sure I'd seen Gimin with Lakon and maybe others down below, just where the inferno was coming from. But what were their chances? I feared for them as much as for us. My chest began to pound. I felt my legs weakening.

'Stay close,' panted Bran as we ran forward. 'We jus' go on. Yahl be with us – there'll be another way. Must be.'

Flames were now licking the floor behind us, searing our heels. We came to a stairwell. Fire was coming up from below. We scrambled up the spiral steps and reached another level, another long curving corridor. From below came the noise of exploding rafters and the crashing of stonework. The floor seemed to heave, as if coming loose from its foundations. We passed a cell, its doors smashed in, empty of occupants. Then another. In it were two bodies: Ferok, with terrible knife wounds. Alongside lay an abandoned rope bundle: salt rope, like the ones Romi had used. Indeed, there was a salty smell in the room. Broken platters and a flagon just like Romi's lay scattered on the floor. I remembered what Romi had told me about his twin, Kami, how the Morok were holding him. Was this his cell? Where was he now?

Bran strode over to the bodies, kicking one. 'Thon knife wounds. I'd recognise 'em anywhere.' Excitement in his voice, he turned to me. 'Tiroc Og's been here. Come, keep goin'. He's in this building somewhere.'

Buoyed up, we raced along the corridor and came to a wooden stairway. At the top was a circular ledge. But it was open on both sides – we were on a sidewall supporting a structure of huge beams and cross timbers. From them hung a huge metal bell, below it a smoke-filled void.

I looked around. Our goal was nearby, a mighty curved building reaching high into the clouds, between us and it a chasm filling with smoke. Behind us the flames were already creeping up the stairs, cracking timbers. There was now *no* way out from here other than down – and certain death.

I turned to look at my friend and at the face of my father. After everything we'd been through, the many close calls, this, then, was surely the end.

The ropes holding the giant bell were already smoking. The timber supports, cooked to combustion by the great heat piling up from below, were beginning to crack. At any moment the bell would fall, taking down the ledge – and probably us – with it.

9

THE BALCONY

'Look there,' shouted Bran, pointing up at the Tor of the Winds. Two figures on a stone balcony were waving wildly: Tiroc Og, still robed as Morc, hood back; another, a bulky figure in Ferok robes who by his size could only be Brach! And there was a third – in sailor's pigtails, busily gathering a huge coil of rope onto the rim. The very image of Romi, but male. Her twin. Kami!

The ledge beneath us was shaking. Suddenly, an arrow thudded deep into the bell support beside us. I looked up to see Tiroc Og kneeling and aiming his bow directly at us. Dangling from the first arrow was a thin rope linked to a bigger one dropping below. Bran, grasping its purpose, dragged up the rope, cut away the string on the arrowhead, handed the thick end to me and said, 'Here, make a closed noose fer yer feet and step in. Yeh go first. Don't worry, I'll bring Faron.'

Another rope came flying over, the arrow thumping beside its twin into the smoking woodwork. Hurriedly, Bran cut the string wrapped the rope coil round Faron's hips, then round his. I hesitated, as yet unable to make out what we were doing.

'Now,' he screamed, 'jump!' and leapt into thin air. It seemed pure madness, jumping into an inferno.

I stood transfixed as they were swallowed up by the smoke and flames. The flames were now above me, licking the top of the huge bell. The cables holding to the roof were snapping away, one after another. Suddenly, the great iron bell flew free from its tethers and plunged below, dragging the timber supports with it, the downwash of air nearly dragging me over. I clutched at the rope as the ledge beneath my feet quaked, then began to give way. It woke me into action.

'Yahl be with us all!' I yelled, launching into the air.

Pummelled with flaming cinders and bits of stones, I plummeted through the smoke, tensing for the impact that must end it all. There was a sudden jolt. I stopped falling and started to go upwards at great speed. Soon the smoke and heat was below and I was being dragged up the stonework of the tor and in seconds, pulled over a balcony ledge and dumped spread-eagled on the floor, numbed with shock. When I looked up, the reassuring face of Tiroc Og was there, holding out his hand and grinning madly. The rope I'd clutched on to for dear life was looped around one of the balcony pillars, still taut, the other end hanging over the balcony. Bran was there, laughing and calmly gathering the rope into coils on the floor.

'Faron?' I exclaimed, shakily standing up. 'Where is he?'

'In there,' Tiroc Og said, nodding towards the room beyond the balcony. I dived in. My father was propped up against a wall, a cup in his hands. 'I've been flying, Osian, like one of them squirrels,' he muttered sleepily. 'Thought I'd never live to see the cub of my old friend, Lir Og. And here with my very own.'

From outside, Bran shouted. 'Tiroc Og, Osian! Give a hand here.' We darted outside to see him struggling amidst a pile of coiled rope holding on to whatever was still over the edge – at the other end of the rope I'd come up on. Grabbing it again, I glanced over the edge and saw the Tarsin I'd seen earlier, clutching at the wall of the tor and anxiously looking down at a figure dangling from a rope below. It was Bron, Bran's twin! In Ferok robes, arms flailing wildly. The rope round his middle had become wedged in a stone projection. The Tarsin was un-roped, clutching the wall, desperately trying to release Bron's rope.

'Pull, with everything yeh have!' shouted Tiroc Og. Bracing my feet against the balcony wall, I heaved and heaved until the rope burned my palms and my shoulders trembled. Slowly, gradually, between the three of us, and with Kami now beside Bron, kicking at the projection, we managed to dislodge the rope and were able to haul the Brach's huge weight up and over the ledge. Kami quickly followed, clambering nimbly over the balcony ledge as if it were just a stair step.

We hugged and greeted them warmly. Kami – it was indeed Romi's twin, freed by Tiroc Og from the cell we'd seen – explained that he'd freefallen with Bron on a rope from the balcony and using the stone pillar as a pulley, had created enough momentum to enable us to be hoisted up after we'd jumped from the Bell Tor. It seemed extraordinarily ingenious, but easy fare, he said, with his seafarer's mastery of ropes and pulleys.

And as for how Bron got there, I was right. I *had* indeed seen our friends running along the side of the courtyard, Gimin with them. Bron explained that Lakon had made the decision to follow us into the Tor of Doors. They'd found Bran's trail of stones, surprised a large posse of Ferok, killed them, taken their robes and split up into small foraging parties. He and the Barod, Yamis, had followed a passage that turned out to be a supply tunnel under the base of the Tor of the Winds. There they bumped by pure chance into Tiroc Og – in the guise of Morc.

I asked about Gimin and the others, a lump in my throat. Bron simply said, 'Osian, my friend, they knows how to look after themselves; they can fight better than anythin' Krachter can throw at 'em. She...' he corrected himself with a chuckle '...*they...* 'll be here somewhere.'

'I saw Yamis. Where is he now?'

'He's in a safe place guarding some of 'em devils that Tiroc Og wanted alive fer questioning,' he replied, turning his attention to take a draught from a water horn.

But I couldn't stop thinking about Gimin. I just had to hope that fortune helped her and the others to negotiate the burning maze of rooms, stairs and corridors we'd just left behind.

Inside, Faron now was sleeping peacefully.

'His injuries? How serious are they?' I asked Tiroc Og.

'Mostly cuts and bruises, but he's very undernourished.'

'You've given him something?' I asked, thinking of one of his herbal infusions.

'Yes, he'll sleep. Easier to carry.'

'Where now – to the Glassin level? How do we get there?' I pressed, adjusting my weapons. 'For Mara and Gwion-Din.'

Tiroc Og seemed reluctant to meet my eye, but answered, 'It's two levels above us. But the way up has been sealed with huge metal doors.'

'Is there another way?' I queried, thinking of the extraordinary way that we'd got to where we were now. If we could get this far... surely, we could get further?

Tiroc Og stood silently, his gaze vacant. None of the others looked in any hurry to move on. Kami, Bran and Bron were seated against a wall, swigging water from their flasks, boasting about their Morok kills. But I was like a branch bent back, ready to spring. I felt like my stomach was going to burst. We'd come so far, been through so much, even saved my father from a cruel death. Mara. Gwion-Din. We were sitting around. Why weren't we racing ahead?

Eventually, Tiroc Og stirred and nodded at Kami. The Tarsin jumped to his feet and began winding and coiling his ropes into piles. Then with a hand on my shoulder, Tiroc Og said to me, 'Patience, my friend, jes' wait a bit. We questioned thon Ferok devil about why yer mother is being held up there, so close to 'em. Well, yeh knows Krachter is after yeh – or rather, that thing yeh carry, yer *Solon*. He'll have figured by now that 'tis us that got into Rakhaus and are behind all the chaos down below. But they have the place surrounded – and think it's a matter of time afore they take back control. Meantimes, what they care about, more than anything, more than the fate of their own, or the fate of their fortress is yer *Solon*. And unless it's delivered up to Kahl, she'll die, most cruelly.'

'They're using her to get to me – and it?' I said, my chest heaving with rage. 'Well, let them have it I say, then...' I burst out, my hand clutching my sword so hard my fingers were white. 'Just tell me what I need to do!'

He put his finger to his lips. 'Certainly not give 'em what they wants.'

I gritted my teeth. 'Not give it up... then *what*...?'

'D'yeh really think they'd take the *Solon*, hand her over safely – and let us all go in peace? Alive? Really?'

I sighed, knowing of course he was right, but still shaking with rage. 'So then, how do we make the rescue?'

'That of course we mus' try. But yeh understand it may be the last thing we do here. Afore I explain, there's somethin' this yeh mus' understand.'

'Yes. What?'

'Look around yeh, Osian. The Tor of Doors is on fire, the Bell Tor's in bits. The building we're in is all that's left of Elvintal. We may have killed hundreds of Morok – maybe thousands, but escape from Rakhaus is only possible if...'

'Cana-Din comes?' I interrupted. This much I understood.

'Yes, without the free tribes 'tis unlikely any of us'll get out of here alive. Yeh jus' don't know what we're dealing with here.'

'But I do, Tiroc Og.'

He looked at me quizzically.

'I saw him, Tiroc Og.'

'Who? Ah, yeh mean Kahl? Him in the balcony above yeh?'

'Yes. The *Solon* sensed his menace.' I remembered the shaft of pain, like nothing I'd ever felt before. 'Felt his presence deep within me, like a tearing of my soul.'

Tiroc Og made a slight nod as if this was no revelation. 'He expected us – remember Garidh's talk of a trap?'

'And, what ... and we're in it now?' I gasped. 'Mara and Faron were just bait?'

'Yes. He knew yeh'd come fer yer kin. Though not how. As fer the havoc we've created below, all that means nothing to Kahl – as long as he gets what he wants.'

'The *Solon.*'

'Yes. And we must make sure he doesn't. I'll tell you this. If he succeeds it's all over fer yer kin, fer yeh, yer brothers and sisters in arms. The time o' the free tribes on this earth will be at an end, gone like the winds in the night desert.'

I gulped at this. It was the first time he'd revealed his full fears about my dangerous acquisition. We'd seen what it could do. In the control of an evil force like Kahl's I knew just how dangerous it could really be. But what was his purpose for it – to use it just to complete his control of Manau? Everyone? Everything? It seemed such a pointless ambition, even fer someone as twisted as the Morok leader.

Or was there something else? A motive stronger than just control? I'd glimpsed his damaged and sightless form under that balcony, felt his terrible presence; but also, maybe prompted by the *Solon*, I'd sensed something else in him, a terrible sadness, a fathomless yearning within that terrible cruelty? And the *Solon*, so terrified. Did it know what his motive was? As for that bird, flying from Krachter to him, a creature that probably followed me from the very outset of my journey, was that a devilish familiar of some kind?

'So, how do we get to Mara?' I blurted out. 'What are our options? There must be a way.'

'Where we are now, Osian, is only part way up the great tor. And as far as I can tell, the three levels below the sky floor are sealed off from the rest of the building, making Kahl and Krachter and the hostages secure from attack. At least this tor cannot catch fire. 'Tis all stone, like thon balcony, even the rafters.'

'But then… there's no way out for them, either.'

He didn't respond. A great weight descended through my frame. I began to shake with tiredness and sorrow. 'So, Tiroc Og,' I said. 'What *do* we do?'

'There is something, my friend, but 'tis up to Kami…' I glanced over at Romi's twin, standing arms folded amidst his neat conical piles of ropes. 'And to yeh…'

'Tell me what I can do – whatever it is, I'll do it!' I burst out.

'It has to do with that which lies in yer *papose*.'

'The *Solon*. But… I have no control it over it. It acts on its own.'

'Yet it seems it *will* act to protect yeh, or itself, whiles yeh carry it.'

'What are you thinking, Tiroc Og?'

'Well, firstly, the only way up to the Glassin Floor is from the outside.'

'You mean… go back out – up that wall?'

He nodded. I stared at him blankly. My stomach heaved with the terrible prospect, yet my heart already began to race. Dreadful though the prospect was, this was something. Probably it would be our final act, where my fate – our fates – would be decided. But I was game and anxious to begin.

'All right, Tiroc Og. Tell me what I need to do.'

10

THE EAGLE

We needed darkness to fall before making our final move. Meantime, Tiroc Og had urged us all – Bron, Kami, Bran and Yamis – to get some rest. We skulked low on that cold balcony, doing our best to stay warm and calm. Faron was asleep. Although dreading the ordeal of being sent back into deep space, I was impatient to begin. Rest was certainly impossible and my mind roamed endlessly over the various mysteries I was wrapped up in, unable to resolve.

Meanwhile thick smoke, dank and pungent with old wood and detritus, was pouring up from the ruined courtyards below, obscuring everything, turning the grey light of day to the colour of sand. The winds howled and shrieked like devils, and I thought of the wild spirits the monks of Elvintal had spent their lives trying to appease. I also thought of that other presence, probably up in the sky somewhere above us, its keen eyes catching our every move: Krachter's eagle.

Seeing me awake, the ever-watchful Tiroc Og said, "'Tis my hope, slender I admit, that with all this smoke, Kahl, Krachter, won't know how close we are. But they'll be prepared for somethin', any roads. In my view 'tis unlikely they'll harm their hostages 'til they have us in their sights.'

'I sometimes wonder if he, Kahl, has just been drawing me – it, the *Solon*, to him.'

'Have yeh considered it might be the other way round, and that's why it's helped keep yeh alive so far?'

'The way the *Solon* reacts when Morok are near would make no sense if that were true. And when I was near Kahl it shivered in terror.'

'Hmmm,' he muttered, resting on his staff and gazing down at the carvings of wild cats. 'But it has never stopped yeh from continuing yer journey into the heart of the beast, or confronting Morok that get in yer way. Could be, I wonders, if it needs yeh to complete a mission, yer mission, and in the end...' he paused.

'In the end?'

'Destroy Kahl!'

I gaped at him open mouthed, wondering how I, we, could ever achieve such a thing.

'The winds 'r gathering,' he said, 'and the light's fading. We needs to wait till 'tis completely dark, so as thon bird cannot see us. Then we makes our move. Meantime, we prepares fer war and fer whatever the fates hand to us – our destinies.'

I swallowed, feeling a bitter chill descend on me. Tiroc Og handed me a bundle of coloured powder capsules then turned away to check on Faron. Bran, Kami and Bron were already mixing powders with water to a paste and were applying it to their faces. I followed their lead, first putting an ash colour on my face, then I made three streaks of colour from ear to ear: red, white and blue, the totem colours of the Alban tribe.

Tiroc Og stood with his back to us, gently murmuring, his hands shivering in the way they had the first time I encountered him, his cat skull staff held at an angle as if addressing the totem, speaking to his ancestors, the green stone at his wrist glittering awhile. Outside, the winds were churning the rising smoke into a whirlpool of suffocating yellow air. Bron handed out dry rations and we sat in silence, me beside Faron, draped in the company's furs and peacefully sleeping. The others sat calmly against the balcony wall, eyes closed, gently murmuring prayers – the final preparations of warriors readying their souls to meet their destinies.

I looked over at the irrepressible Yamis, who somehow was to carry Faron with us – dried Morok blood mixing with the war colours on his face. I thought of his tribe and their great gentility and warm manners – forced against their nature by circumstance to become killers, but their build and solid frames making them an implacable foe. Would he, they, I wondered, ever be able to return to their old, gentle ways?

My own destiny and the fate of my kin, it seemed, more than ever, inextricably tied up with that of the *Solon*, this curious thing that had become part of my mission, from which I could not be separated. Now Tiroc Og seemed to be setting our success on it. But whether its powers were a match for Kahl's sorcery... well, I had my doubts, given its terror when we'd been in the near vicinity of the Morok leader. It was as if he and I had a shared history – and we were now approaching some kind of fork in the path of that history, whether for ill or good.

My thoughts returned to Krachter's eagle. I'd only ever experienced its kind in the form of the white eagles of Alba, our fellow hunters in the high hills behind our home. They were wind soarers that lived for thousands of moons, watching down us from great heights. They'd come down when we'd gone, looking for easy pickings after a kill. Like the wild cats and wolves of the hills, they had their place in the great scheme of the wild – and in our lives. We used their discarded feathers for our headdresses and pinned them to our festive robes. Occasionally one of the tribes would find an abandoned juvenile and tame it to catch small game. Glorious creatures, their snow-white plumage flecked with sungold – coloured thus because it is said their ancestors flew with the gods.

But once we came across an eagle that was not Albin white. Grandfather and I had been hunting in the hills and we'd turned for home in the twilight when we came across a flat clearing in the heights, a stone circle in its midst. Grandfather, I could tell, was looking at it with a view to setting up camp. We stretched our bender skin between the stones for cover and lit a fire to roast a game bird we'd caught. My aunt would worry that we had not returned, but she knew I was in capable hands. I loved the excitement of a night on the hill and wrapped warm in furs by the fire I eagerly looked forward to our dinner.

Until suddenly, in the fading light, Grandfather started to behave strangely, stopping what he was doing and loudly chanting the names of gods; something he only ever did when danger, usually a storm, was imminent.

'What's up, Grandfather?' I asked, feeling anxious.

In reply he pointed up to the heavens. There, in the distance, its wings tipped blood red from the last rays of the setting sun, was a huge wind soarer. Only this one was jet black, and easily twice the size of the Albin white eagles. The circles it was making were small and its head was pointed down straight at us. It was as if there was an invisible tunnel between us. We were being watched!

'I don't understand, Grandfather,' I said. 'It's just an eagle.'

'No, Osian. That's not just an eagle. It's a *drein*. It doesn't fly with the gods but with the very devils,' he replied tersely, and with a look on his face as if he knew this eagle.

He was shaken, pale even. Suddenly, he began taking down the bender and kicking snow over the fire. 'Forget your weariness, Grandson. We have to be gone from here.' I knew not to question his decision, though I was tired and hungry.

Later, when we'd scrambled through snowdrifts down the mountain in ominous silence and the fires of our lakeside homes were in sight, I gathered up the courage to break into his thoughts. 'What is a *Drein*, Grandfather?'

His reply was terse. 'It's a companion to sorcerers, Osian. A bird of ill omen.'

And now I knew that the eagle hovering above us, the one I'd seen with Krachter and the one I saw with Grandfather, was the same, a *drein*. Kahl's *drein*. Its sighting up here, and its sighting of us, in this terrible place, was not a good omen. Both back then and now.

Tiroc Og emerged from his trance, bowed his head towards his staff, then nodded to Kami, who rose to his feet. Then, hand on my shoulder, he said, 'Osian, my friend. It's time,' and took up an end of one of Kami's ropes.

I looked at the rope and into his eyes, at the cat-like pupils larger than usual – and held my breath. But the tone of his explanation for what was to come was matter of fact: 'Kami will make yeh ready with this end of his rope. Then he'll climb the wall and get as far as he can using the smoke as cover. When he's above it, he'll drive two barbed bolt hooks deep into the stone. Through one he'll thread the other end of this rope and his own and tie himself off on the other side of the hooks. He'll then drop suddenly back to us and deep below. The force of this'll sling yeh up into the mighty winds as far as thon hook. Jes' wait fer the impact and use yer legs against the wall to steady yerself. Then yeh're in the place where Kami has just come from. He'll have stopped falling by then and 'll climb back up to us. Trust in him. D'yeh see it, so far?'

Kami had already begun wrapping the rope round my hips and thighs to form a harness. And a waist band to which were attached balls of strong thin woven cord. Doing my best to suppress my fears, I replied, 'I understand. It'll be like a pulley. He comes down, I go up. When I get there, what next?'

He handed me a goat crook and a quiver of cross bolts and replied, 'There's a lightning rod hangs out over the top of the tor – above where we are. Yeh'll be able to see it in the thin air up there. From the hook yeh're on, yeh must attach the loops at the bottom of these bolts to the ends of the string balls and fire 'em up the side of the tor till one of 'em drops over the rod and swings back to yeh. Catch it wi' this 'ere crook. If yeh miss the rod jes' cut the string with yer knife. Jes' let it go. If yeh get one over and can catch it, tie it to the second rope that Kami has placed up there, then pull the string so the rope goes over the lightning rod and back down. Pull that rope through the second bolt hook and tie it off. That's the one we'll all use to get us up to the top o' the tor.'

'What if I'm spotted? We saw Krachter's eagle earlier – what if it sees me, sees what I'm doing?'

'Watch fer it. If yeh see it, yeh must kill it!'

How? I looked at him aghast. In these conditions? Up there, dangling from the side of a tor, strings and ropes everywhere, winds no doubt buffeting me around, how could I hit a distant moving target?

'Yeh've no choice. If the gods are with yeh… and yer *Solon*, yeh will… yeh must succeed!' he replied, with a conviction quite out of keeping with the task he was setting me.

But, taking a slow breath to calm my beating heart, I looked him in the eye and said, 'Your faith in me… is undeserved. My tribe do not easily take to the air – and I am not a great archer such as yourself.'

I felt a tremor of shame when he did not reply. It must have looked like cowardice and so I spoke formally. 'The life that is in me is in the hands of my good friends and it is given freely. I am in your debt. But how can I promise success?'

'There is reason in yeh doing it, Osian,' he replied reassuringly, hand again on my shoulder. 'Yeh're masterly with yer sling, young 'un. If the bird appears, yeh must use it as soon as it does. Thon black devil may be the master of these airs, but I believes yer slingshot is equal to it. An arrow fired even by me in these howling winds wouldn't make a moving target. Yer sling stone is sure – I've seen it. But still yeh'll need to allow a little fer the wind – blowin' easterly at the moment, I can see.'

'And if I don't succeed?'

He sighed and gripped my shoulder tight. 'I'm countin' on it comin' straight fer yeh – to get to yer papose. Yeh have yer knife – if it comes, remember it'll come straight fer yer eyes. Maybe though yer *Solon* 'ill help yeh – to keep it from being taken.'

The mysterious power of the *Solon* or not, what were my real chances? I pondered the terrifying prospect of dangling from a rope from a precipice nearer to the sky than the earth, my eyes stinging from a smoke storm in winds that could take your skin off. This was a slender thread for all our fortunes to hang from. But I had no choice. What of Mara – and Gwion-Din and my companions – were I to fail?

I must have looked doubtful, for Tiroc Og, as if reading my thoughts, spoke emphatically. 'Trust in my instincts. 'Tis our best chance; I cannot think of gettin' to yer kin, and us gettin' out of here alive any other way.'

Kami, who'd been waiting patiently alongside, put his hand on my arm and spoke up. 'Courage, young 'un,' he said. 'Think of me bein' tossed aroun' in a crow's nest in a gale – wi' mighty winds and hunderd foot waves in a leakin' Aguan ship. Against that, this 'ere is nuthin'. And 'member ol' Romi. I know yeh think she betrayed yeh, but in the end gave the very life in her, so yeh could go on.'

I gazed over at Faron, peacefully asleep, and at Bran, who returned my gaze. His eyes were watering. My eyes moistened too, thinking it unlikely I'd ever see any of them again. My own fate now was of little concern. I was doing this for my kin and for the friends I'd come here with, who'd risked their own lives to help me in my impossible quest. And I determined, clenching my fist, I *would* succeed.

'Consider it done, my friends,' I said, smiling weakly. 'The attempt, anyway.' I handed Tiroc Og my sword and staff. 'I may not be needing these.' I had my sling in my cloak and a crook, my knife, a quiver of bolts at my waist and my crossbow round my shoulders. It was enough.

'Said like the great warrior yeh've proved to be, Osian,' replied Tiroc Og, smiling warmly. 'I'll take care of these for yeh – and remember we're behind yeh all the way.'

I considered asking him to take a message to Gimin, a farewell. Instead, I kissed the rope harness and uttered a silent prayer to the great Otar father and mother of our own race, for the safety of the beautiful Fox-Wolf and for all. Then I stepped against the balcony rail, sling armed in one hand; crossbow, quiver of bolts, pouch of slingstones and a spool of leader rope at my belt. No bothersome Ferok robe, just my knife in my *papose*. And alongside it, the *Solon*, as yet unresponsive to the terrifying prospect I was about to subject us to.

'When yeh get yer bolt over the lightning rod,' said Tiroc Og, 'pull three times on the rope yer on. This'll be the signal for us to come after yeh – with Kami's help. Hopefully the winds up there and the smoke below 'ill drive our scents away from any of 'em flyin' devils keepin' watch. They'll not be in too much of a hurry to fly in thon gale.'

I'd forgotten about those other flying creatures, the Skarag, Kahl's vicious dragons, but I'd seen none since Krater Lake.

Kami had already climbed on to the balcony, ready to begin his ascent, one length of rope in his teeth, the other round his waist, the two great coils on the floor behind me beginning to unwind like waking snakes. Strapped to his belt was a razor sharp cutlass. I held my breath as he warned us to keep well clear from the coils, muttered a prayer, then, seemingly unbothered by the freezing wind that battered against the tor, was gone, the ropes on the floor whipping past our faces.

It seemed like the longest wait before they stopped uncurling. Each swirl of smoke that curled up from below and gust of wind over the edge pressed home the horror of what I was about to do. Tiroc Og had given me a foul smelling infusion, saying, 'This keeps out the cold. Works from the inside, and t'will give yeh courage.' I threw it back, coughing with the bitter taste. Instantly a fresh warmth gathered in my stomach and spread to my fingertips and toes; a gentle tingling that seemed to enhance their sensitivity. I felt grateful for any help it could give. At Tiroc Og's signal, I climbed on to the balcony and waited.

Suddenly, my rope went tight. With a violent jolt I soared into the sky, swinging in a maelstrom of smoke and screaming wind, emptiness below and above. Strange to say, my terror was mingled with another sensation. For the third time in my brief life, I was flying like a bird and scary as it was, I felt the freedom of the air.

A blurry grey shape plummeted past me, dropping like a stone into the yellow smoke: Kami. Then in seconds, I came to a sudden juddering stop. My knees, raised in the air by the harness, crashed into the jagged side of the tor with a brief but real stab of pain. I braced against the wall with my legs and took a deep calming breath. The air was indeed thinner up here and there was no smoke, but the light was darkening into night. I was dangling from one of two barbed spikes hammered deep into the stone face. Seeing this gave me enough confidence to push a little away from the wall for a better view above.

As I swung out, I felt resistance from below. It meant that Kami had successfully tied off at the balcony. I looked up and glimpsed the lightning bar, a long dark rod with three or maybe four branches, spread out like the fingers of an outstretched hand, wavering in the winds. There was no sign of the eagle – or any Skarag.

I armed my sling and tucked it into my belt so that it was reachable in one move. I then selected one of Tiroc Og's looped bolts from the quiver and taking my crossbow off my shoulder – it seemed heavier than usual – firmly attached the loose end of one of the leader strings to the bolt loop. Then I swung out again from the wall, aimed upwards and allowing for the wind, I fired.

The bolt sped through the firmament, wavering in the blasts, the spool at my waist whirring furiously as the leader string snaked through the air. But instead of flying true to its target, to my horror it curved mid-flight towards the tor wall, smashed against it side on and hovered in the air, ready to drop back down. Then, in a freak wind, incredibly, as if a hand had grabbed it, the bolt seemed to take fresh position, the pointed end speeding smoothly upwards and arching over the lightning rod before dropping back down. It couldn't have run more perfectly. Indeed, it wasn't possible. And yet it had happened.

I watched on in amazement as the bolt descended, buffeted by the wind against the tor wall, then slid down the last few lengths against the stone before coming to a shuddering halt just beneath my feet, the spool having fully run out. I hadn't even needed to use the crook.

With freezing fingers, I fumbled the end of Kami's second rope through the loop on the second spike, tied it tightly to the string that had come down, then began to pull on the other end attached to the spool so that the rope rose up and over the lightning rod. It was slow work and, swaying about in the wind, I needed to use both hands and all my attention for the task.

The eagle! I heard it before I saw it: the sharp screech of a bird of prey. And then it was on me, outstretched claws inches from my face, behind them the yellow eye, the white stripe, the open beak, ready to gouge and rip.

Suddenly there came a flash like a lightning strike and the air shimmered green. The bird froze, wings outstretched suspended in space, inches from my head; the claws, the beak, splayed in the attack, but unmoving. But I *could* move and I kicked myself off the wall, reaching for my sling.

But abruptly the flash passed. The bird's foul breath was on me, a smell of carrion, a flurry of dark feathers. I managed to swing away as a talon tore across the skin of my forehead. I felt a brief, burning pain. The bird continued a downward curve, swooped up away from the wall, then wheeled back on itself and rose above me, screeching, extending its claws – straight for my eyes.

Blood poured down my face, obscuring my vision. Blindly I fired my sling, just glimpsing the stone passing through a wing tip, dislodging some feathers. I'd missed! But it was enough to drive the bird away. Wiping my eyes, I looked about. But it had gone.

The wind meanwhile had risen again and battered me against the tor, nearly tearing me from my harness, the ropes and strings flying wildly. I clutched the wall and began again pulling on the string. At last, the rope began to appear. So far, I'd succeeded.

But the bird returned, reappearing as a thin dark line in the distance, growing as it came towards me. It was flying sidelong: an impossible target in a maelstrom. It had to be right on me if there was to be any possibility of me getting a direct hit.

I readied the sling cord and held it to my eye.

The bird came. This time though there was no murmur from the *Solon*, no green flash, no suspension of time. I was on my own. And it was almost on me.

I fired.

I heard a great whack and a screech. I'd struck the bird full on the chest. I saw the surprise in its eyes, a flash of hatred. This would have been a mortal blow for any earthly creature. But this was a *drein* and still it came at me. And I was undefended. Uselessly, I raised my arm over my face. But too late.

11

THE TOR OF THE WINDS

A morass of feathers obliterated everything. I felt its talons dropping down my cheek and a searing pain, a jarring in my neck, blood everywhere, the breath knocked out of me, my nose filled with the huge creature's stink. I cried out in shock, my voice lost in the winds screaming around the tor. I was pinned against the stone; only my *papose* stopping me being crushed by the sheer force of the huge bird crashing into me.

But the bird was dead.

I caught my breath and muttered thanks to Yahl for my life. The corpse of the *drien* – if that's what it was – slid down my chest and dropped away, its limp form tossed about by the wind as it tumbled down. Incredibly, my shot had found its mark. And although I was the instrument of its death, once again I realised that I'd been helped by the *Solon*, acting through me – and so far, once again, *for* me.

I wiped our mingled life-bloods and its feathers off my face and pulled three times on the rope that held me to the wall. Kami was soon below my feet, bouncing up the wall anchored to the second rope and in seconds was alongside, his great clawed mitts making quick work of an otherwise impossible ascent. 'Yeh did right by thon critter,' he yelled above the blast, thumping me on the shoulder. 'Now we've to get ourselves up to the top. Are yeh goin' to be all right to mak' the moves? Yeh're a brave one, that's fer sure.'

'Just give me a breath, Kami,' I answered, still shaking.

'I'm goin' to put in another spike, Osian, so I can bring up the chief. Then the three of us can go,' he said before he started hammering.

'What about Bran and Bron?'

'I wouldn't have the sea power to belay either of 'em,' he answered, attaching another rope to his new spike.

I took a deep breath at the prospect of the ascent to come. My stomach was already churning. Us against how many – and against *what?* And no Bran to watch my back.

'I'll drop down now,' he said and was away, giving no time for a parting message for Bran and Faron.

Death had stared me in the eye many times on my journey to this place. But surely, now, in this most unlikely of situations and so close to my goal, it would have its hour.

Tiroc Og was quickly alongside and speaking. 'What yeh've done on this day is truly remarkable, Osian.' Then, more sombrely, he added, 'When Kami rejoins, the two of yeh needs pull on this rope to get me to the roof. When I'm there I can assist Kami to get yeh up, then he'll climb up to join us.' Then, tying off the rope he'd come up on, he took the rope hanging over the lightning rod and wrapped it round his middle. 'Yeh did well, Osian, against thon devil, no doubt. Means we still have the possibility of surprise.'

'No Bran with us, though.'

'I'm hoping we can let our friends in once we're inside,' he replied, pointing to the thunderstick at his belt.

'What will be up there, Tiroc Og?' I asked, almost fearful to ask. Skarag?

'There's a platform, small-walled, put there by the monks to stop them being blown off by the winds when they came up to hang prayer flags and lay out their dead fer the soarers. Here, give a hand,' he said, tugging Kami's rope to help quicken the agile Tarsin ascent up the stone. Once with us it was time for the final haul to the top. It wasn't far, but nonetheless daunting, like we were entering the heavens. Tiroc Og didn't want to risk the belaying with a sudden appearance at the top, so with Kami and I hauling and him using his clawed mitts to stay close to the tor wall, he clambered slowly up and over on to the roof.

There was an anxious moment when he did not at first reappear. But thankfully, his head popped over and he signalled for us to follow. Holding my breath, I allowed myself to be hauled up on the belay loop over the rod; Tiroc Og pulling from above and Kami from below. I was soon there with Kami quickly following in a frenzy of clambering and roping. We were atop the Tor of Winds: three of us now against our enemies, presumably skulking in a lair below us, but with numbers of guards and forces unknown, hopefully unaware of our presence – and proximity?

It was bitterly cold. Thick fogs of cloud, shoved about by the squalls, flew about, the damp air penetrating my skin, creeping right into my bones. Visibility was almost nothing. The squalls were beginning to settle to a low, eerie howl, as if waiting for something to happen. Tiroc Og was the first to spot it – pointing north where loomed the outline of a massive jet-black storm-cloud, crackling with lightning. 'I don't believe it,' he whispered. 'A Helm! Of all times. Yahl save us.'

On our knees, hugging the floor against the squalls, we surveyed our near surroundings. Poles bearing the tattered remnants of prayer flags rose out of a high walled enclosure in the centre of the roof. From the near side protruded the great stone that anchored the lightning rod. Underneath was fixed a box with mesh sides, of which one side was open, littered with straw and a scattering of small bones – the roost for the *dreich* I'd killed. Crawling towards it, we came to a massive metal trapdoor, around it piles of slimy greenish lizard dung, the first indication of the presence of Skarag. Then, led by Tiroc Og, we crept around the far side of the walled enclosure. Here was a passage into the enclosure. We went through and came to a series of steps going downwards into the tor. This, he signalled, was our way in.

Dipping into his long pack he passed us some vials and said, 'Drink this. I've saved it specially. A gift from Aehmir. It contains *soma*, the food of the fighting gods. 'Twill warm the body, fill yer spirits with ardour, and protect yeh against marsh gas – but main thing it'll help yeh see in the dark. 'Tis cat-sight!'

Drinking it back, I felt a rush of energy course through my body; a warm glow emanating from my skin. To my amazement, I suddenly no longer felt the cold. And indeed, I could see around me, not daylight clear – but the outline of things, a soft yellow light like an aura around everything.

The dampness in my bones had abated, yet still I shivered, haunted by a doubt, the probability that we were in fact stumbling headlong like blind mice into a trap as yet unsprung. We'd made it to Rakhaus, in the process destroying large parts of Kahl's fortress, killing many Morok, freeing two captives and foiling their execution. Krachter and Kahl certainly knew rebel foes had got into the complex of tors. Kahl had "seen" me earlier and probably sensed the presence of the *Solon*, as it had him making me a mere ploy in some kind of cosmic struggle between him and it.

If there was purpose in it all, whose purpose was being served? For all that it had enabled me to do, for all the curious interventions, the *Solon* was an inanimate object, not *alive* in any way that I or even shrewd Tiroc Og knew. My own mission here had been to find and bring home my kin and so far, the *Solon* had made it possible for me to get this far. But whatever we achieved, up here we remained surrounded by Morok forces, rushing no doubt towards the tor from all parts of the island. How on Yahl's earth would we, my kin, my friends, ever be able to leave – alive?

Then, as all these thoughts and fears merged into one, I felt in my young bones that Kahl knew exactly where we were now and that we were coming. If so, with his powers, why would he let us get so close?

Kami meanwhile had been carefully laying out his ropes in coils within the protective edge of the roof enclosure. Were we to survive, we'd need them to get back down – unless of course there was another way? Tiroc Og was scratching his chin, something I noticed he did in advance of any major decision, weighing up the odds as a cat might do as it contemplated the position – and maybe threat level – of a rival or a prey hidden in foliage. Did the shrewd Wildcat shaman think we were walking into a trap?

Then, he simply said, 'We go down in.'

Bows armed, swords held out, we crept towards the entrance. Kami took position behind me and although he didn't give me the comfort of Bran's huge form, his strength was surely Bran's equal: his shoulders were huge from a life of hauling ship rope and beams and his clawed webbed mitts were weapons in themselves. But he was sprightlier than the Brach and though I'd not seen him in action, I could imagine the terror and carnage he could unleash with his cutlass, now held in readiness. Over one shoulder hung a small rope, one end tied to his wrist, the other ended in a noose. This wasn't a climbing rope – this was a weapon!

The steps down ended in a metal door. Tiroc Og tentatively pulled a handle in the middle. It opened easily. Too easily? There was a flicker of red light beyond. We crept soundlessly down another series of steps to another curving level, all empty, on one side a great flat wall that seemed to cut the disc shape of the tor in half. We were on one side, the wall separating us from the second half. From somewhere drifted a bad smell that reminded me of the cavern, and my first sighting of Skarag.

Suddenly, the *Solon* began quivering at my back. Danger – nearby! My heart began to pound.

At the far end of the level lay a trapdoor made of planks lying slightly ajar, like a bad fit, or broken. Red light – firelight – filtered through the gap. From below came a murmur of voices, too muffled for me to make out.

Tiroc Og tested the handle on the trapdoor, moving it up a fraction, closed it and turned. 'Damp yer kerchiefs and put 'em on,' he whispered, dropping water from his drinking horn on to his cloth and wrapping it round his face. Then, signalling to us to stand on either side of the trapdoor, he took out from his robe a slender green firestick – a type I hadn't seen before. Sparking the fuse, he yanked up the trapdoor, threw down the stick, slammed down the trap, leapt back and shouted, 'Quick. Lie flat!'

Almost immediately, a battery of barbed crossbolts smashed through the wood from below and came to a juddering halt, lethal points sticking through. They were purple tipped. Poisonous! The enemy had been waiting for us!

A thin, greenish vapour drifted out of the gap, rose up and was soon gone. Marsh gas.

'Wait!' Tiroc Og said. 'Let the rest of the vapour escape.'

But no more gas or bolts followed. He lowered his kerchief, sniffed the air then, sword in hand, rubbed the green stone at his wrist, muttered an invocation and whispered, 'Follow when I say.' Then, replacing his mask, he lifted back the hatch and climbed down.

We waited for what seemed like an age, both stunned with apprehension, hearing nothing and were just about to disobey and go down when he emerged and said, 'follow.' At the bottom of the steps lay an anteroom of some kind. And there a grim sight greeted us. Three Red Skraeling guards lay on the floor, silent, immobile, their throats cut. There was blood everywhere. A fourth sat against a wall, a great wound on his head, tied and gagged, eyes wide in terror, the eyeballs bulging out of bony sockets. The gas had allowed Tiroc Og to do his grisly work.

'Shhh, don't speak!' he whispered, indicating a metal door at the end of the anteroom. 'There's another guardroom beyond. This piece of vermin,' he said, 'told me, in return fer keepin' his eyes, that there's five more of 'em through there. Krachter, it seems, is just below here, on the Glassin floor with Mara, Gwion-Din and more Skraeling – don't know how many. Thon doorway opens, but the entrance to the Glassin floor, I'm told, can only be opened from the inside.'

'So how do we get in?' I mouthed.

'First, we have to deal with the devils in there.' He held up another of the thin sticks and said, 'We'll have to use this. I'm 'fraid 'tis my last one. Masks on. Yeh ready? Let's go.'

We followed him across the room to the doorway. Producing from his long pack a tiny mirror he wedged it in his staff, held the mirror over the gap at the bottom of the door, glanced at it, calmly lit another gas stick and shoved it under the gap.

No reaction from inside... then sounds of crashing and thumping. Tiroc Og put the mirror back at the gap and peered at it. Then, after a short wait he nodded to us and gently pulled the handle, a fraction at first, then more. The door opened easily. Too easily. Still no reaction from inside.

Cautiously, we opened the door and, masks on, went in. Four Red Skraeling were spreadeagled on the ground, a clutter of cooking and eating apparatus scattered about. We'd disturbed their meal! The gas had mostly dissipated but at the far end a patch remained and appeared to be dissolving up into some kind of flue. Suddenly, something whipped past my ear: a flying rope. A single Red Skraeling

150

emerged from the shadows, masked, and wielding a crossbow, but already faltering. Kami's lasso, tight round his neck, was bringing him to the ground, sending his weaponry clattering at our feet. Three more appeared, all masked, racing towards us with barbed maces and curved swords. But not for long. Tiroc Og's arrow was in the chest of the first, the second dropped with a knife at his throat, while Kami had the last, cutlass thrown like a dart into its face. It all happened so quickly, in a blur of motion, I didn't even have time to fire my slingshot.

The green gas had gone, but the far end of the room was still in shadow. I saw movement, a glance of a sword tip. I pulled back my crossbow, but almost immediately faltered. The face that emerged was not like the others. It was a Skraeling, but female, mask down, standing blinking at the bolt I was about to unleash. She was skeletal like the others but had beautiful, great doe eyes and a mane like silver, tossed back. She'd lowered her sword; tears were rolling down her face. Automatically, I began to lower my bow.

'Don't!' screamed Tiroc Og. But a curved blade was already scything towards me. I jumped away. It glanced off my side, the force enough to slice through the thickest part of Kami's harness, which dropped away. Her face became ugly, filled with rage; her body twisted like a spinning top and I saw the flash of another weapon, a knife. But it never flew. My bolt had struck her right in the chest. She dropped to her knees, then began to slowly crumble as her life force melted away, her eyes boring into mine, curses spitting from her lips.

When I looked around, all the Red Skraeling in the room had been dispatched by my companions, including the one that Tiroc Og had questioned. He still had his eyes – but they stared vacantly into space.

Indicating us forward, Tiroc Og led us into the shadows – a stairwell curving downwards. My fingers traced the curved edges of the tor as we descended. But at the bottom we found only a dead end.

We could go no further. Tiroc Og ran his hands over the wall, nails scratching at the surface, and whispered, 'There's not even a doorway, just solid stone.'

'What do we do?'

We were so near to our goal, or so I'd thought; yet could go no further.

'We've two options, Osian,' he replied. 'We either go back up and try to enter through the other trapdoor – the one used by the Skarag, or...'

'Could we blast our way through here with thundersticks?' I interrupted.

'Ah, my friend. To use them here would be dangerous. The shockwave would kill everyone beyond – including Mara, if she be there; and probably take half the tor with it – along with us. So...' he muttered, pacing backward and forwards, deep in concentration. He'd got us all so far... there'd be a plan of some kind.

Kami and I exchanged troubled glances, then the old seadog smiled at me. He was irrepressible, just like Romi, his twin.

'Tiroc Og, you said "Or..."?'

Putting his hand on my shoulder, Tiroc Og spoke. 'I believe the time has come. Time to test your weapon, to make use of its destiny, its *almadh*.'

'What d'yeh mean, Chief?' asked Kami.

'My friend,' he responded, 'our little brother has in his possession a *sidhir*, which Kahl dearly wants – no doubt fer its destructive power.'

The word meant little to me. But clearly it meant something shocking to Kami, for he took a step away, muttering, 'Yahl save us! Demons 'o the deep! Evil 'gainst evil. T'will sink our ship, I tell yeh; take us down with it.'

I was reminded of Romi – her fear of the *Solon*, her look of terror, not relief, when against all odds and with the *Solon*'s help, the tables had been turned against Garidh.

'Tis a chance we must take, Kami,' replied Tiroc Og. 'The best cure for venom is venom itself. Here it could well be last weapon in our armoury. Kahl, Krachter – they have to be beaten… whatever the cost to us. It is what Romi would have wished, were she with us today.'

'What can this thing do, Chief?' asked Kami, his voice faltering.

'Likes yeh fears, it can summon up forces beyond mortal ken. But I'm hoping it'll help take us into the Glassin floor, without killing us – and our friends.'

Kami still looked worried. I too was concerned, but not on account of superstition.

'Tiroc Og, I too have concerns. Remember, I've no control over it,' I said. 'I cannot tell it what to do. It has its own way.'

'Till now, it has not let yeh die – it seems its instinct is to keep yeh – itself – from the claws of the Morok. Yet strangely it's helped bring yeh here. There must be purpose to it – lettin' itself be taken into the very bosom of the enemy. If we're to die in the end, then so be it. Let it seek its *almadh* – its destiny – fer it may be our *almadh*! It must be used – fer the sake of all.'

'But use it – how?'

'Bring it out, Osian. We've tarried too long,' he said firmly.

Reluctantly, I reached into my *papose*. Kami backed away, shaking his head, muttering as I pulled it out. Then, seeing the sign of the Morok branded on its side, he groaned again. 'Tis an enemy thing. Yahl save us.'

'The *sidhir* is locked inside,' said Tiroc Og reassuringly. 'That's only a Morok outer seal yeh see, Kami. They'd stolen it, yer thing of power, or sorcery as some would see it. Now Osian, yeh must talk to it, to yer *Solon* as yeh call it. Tell it what it must do – break down the barrier ahead, take us through.'

'I've never asked anything of it before. And I can't explain how it talks to me, helps me. It's all feelings and impulses. How can I tell it anything?'

'Use yer will. *Will* what yeh want it to do,' he urged, his voice raised, almost chant-like. 'Will it, harder than anything ever before. Will for yer mother's life, yer father, yer brothers and sisters who've risked their lives to be here... and fer the soul of Romi who saved yeh. Will for the young life in yeh too. Whatever yer *Solon* is, I believes it hates the Morok as much as we do, wants to destroy them as much as us.'

I held it out in my arms. Though slight in size and weight, in the flickering light of the fire it felt heavy, larger than it looked, even menacing. And as we watched, it seemed to pulse and swell, as if anticipating what was going to happen next. Though unchanged in size it had a feel of something bigger than myself, bigger than Kami or Tiroc Og, bigger than our giant friends Bran and Bron, the stone door below us – as big as the tor. It vibrated, but slightly and unlike ever before, this movement was visible to all.

Kami cried out, covering his eyes. 'Yahl save us all – 'tis dark magik. 'Tis a ting bigger than the seas theyselves.'

'Do it, Osian. Do it!' Tiroc Og shouted. 'Will it to act!'

I closed my eyes and thought about how it had come to me, the silver light on the water, beckoning me, then how it had bonded, become a part of me, an extra limb, yet with a determination of its own. I thought of what might lie beyond us, how we so badly needed to get through. I tried to visualise what might lay inside that dark seal. Tried hard. At first, nothing. I thought of the last time I'd seen that silver shape – the moon, shining like a beacon over the trees on the Isle of the Dead, its majestic beauty, its silvern serenity. The image of the moon in my head seemed to grow bigger and bigger and I felt the *Solon* go warm in my hands, like it was responding. Then, I breathed in deeply and as Tiroc Og had instructed, *willed* it to destroy the barrier. 'Destroy it,' I muttered as I emptied my lungs and opened my eyes.

Suddenly, something was happening. It felt like the lungs of the world were emptying. An image of a storm at sea flashed before me. A great wave rose and rushed at us, threatening to overwhelm us. Suddenly it parted and a tall thin figure emerged from the gap. The eyes were unseeing, the mouth was set in a mocking, taunting grimace. Three talons pointed straight at me, one curving inwards. 'Mine!' screamed a broken voice.

Kahl! His? The *Solon* was his! But… it couldn't be…

I fell back. Darkness enveloping me, so that I couldn't even see my companions. My head reeled with thoughts, with shock. Tiroc Og had been right. It had been his. It had been lost to him. He wanted it back; was even prepared to see the destruction of his headquarters, of his army and his allies, of everything, to secure it.

Was this what the *Solon* wanted too? I knew it feared him but was it like a dog that feared its master. Kahl? Had I been beguiled by it – to bring it back to him? Surely not.

'No!' I cried out. 'It shall not be. No… No!'

At this a great noise, a drone rose out of the darkness, followed by an ear-shattering blast, as if all the winds upon the earth had gathered together and crashed into one another. My ears ached; my head reeled. A great searing heat overwhelmed me. Something seemed to leap out from inside me: a flash like a bolt of lightning. There was an explosion of light and noise and I felt I was flying.

12

THE STORMING

My companions were crouching, covering their heads. A cascade of stone and shards of wood was peppering the stairwell above us, followed by a cloud of dust and smoke that gathered and clotted then flew up and away, passing us all by as if we were in a bubble of protective air. I was on my knees, the *Solon* cradled in my arms, vibrating wildly like a terrified animal. I couldn't tell if it was I or it that trembled the most. There was a great hole in the wall and a stairwell going down and we were all standing staring at it, transfixed by what had happened.

'Go!' screamed Tiroc Og, the first to move, half-dragging a shaken Kami behind him down the stairwell. Hardly able to get myself upright, I fumbled the *Solon* back into my *papose* and followed with unsteady steps. Stumbling over debris, we arrived at the threshold of a large circular chamber. Skraeling guards lay lifeless all over the floor before us. Blood everywhere.

At the back of the chamber, a tall cloaked Ferok was staggering to his feet, disbelief on his face. An eyepatch. Krachter! He grabbed a shield off a wall and screamed, 'Kill them!' Two Red Skraeling stumbled chaotically out of the shadows but Tiroc Og was on them in an instant, a whirlwind of fury, Morok mace in one mitt, his demonic sword in the other, dispensing death before they could lift their weapons.

I fired a bolt at Krachter, but it bounced uselessly off the shield. Two more guards appeared but were quickly disabled by a single throw of Kami's lasso, the noose tightening round their necks, binding them together like wheat sheaves. Immobilised, they were dragged to the ground, coughing for breath. Their last breath.

Krachter, meanwhile, had disappeared through a side passage. I gave chase, loading my sling as I ran, then found myself on the threshold of a fire lit chamber with a large window to one side and beyond, another stairwell.

A drawn, aged Eronn lay sprawled over a rough bedframe. Krachter was at the back of the room, dragging a hooded figure towards a stairwell. I aimed my sling at his head. But he had a dagger at his captive's throat. It was Mara! Her face was deadly white, yet her head held high and proud. 'Osian, my son!' she shouted. I kept my sling raised but his head was behind hers. Were my aim even slightly out, she would be dead.

Terrified by our sudden, violent appearance, he showed every sign of panic, eyes darting here and there, a sliver of foam dripping from his mouth. 'Don't try to follow, dog!' he yelled in Ironese, dragging Mara backwards into the darkness. 'Osian!' she called, struggling and kicking. 'Don't come after me. Look to yourself. Save Faron. Help Gwion-Din...' The rest was lost; his hand was over her mouth.

'That's a stair – it goes back to the roof,' shouted Tiroc Og. 'Kami, go with him. I'll follow.'

I dashed into the stairwell and saw a flash of blue robe disappearing above. From behind came a crash of glass, followed by the sound of howling wind, then the unmistakeable echoing of a conch. Tiroc Og was calling out through the Glassin window!

I glanced back. Kami was there. 'Go careful, young 'un,' he whispered. 'I'm with yeh.'

At the top of the stairs was a metal hatch. I pushed on it, gently at first, then hard, but it didn't budge. I yelled aloud in frustration. 'Yer weapon,' Kami shouted, 'Use it again. Use it!'

I reached into my *papose* and pulled out the *Solon*. Once again, I willed it to help us. The drone rose gradually at first. 'Get back down, Kami, cover yer ears,' I shouted. We slid back round the spiral. Just in time, for the explosion that followed sent metal shards deep into the stonework around. Abandoning caution, we rushed up. The trapdoor was no more, above it another level, a dark space, reeking of excrement; winds from above howling through it. Then the screeching. Skarag!

There was no time to feel fear. We hauled ourselves up and dived into the darkness. Lizard eyes met us, barely visible in the darkness, but I made out the shapes of their leathery forms slithering away, howling in terror and pain. The floor was sticky underneath our feet, wet with ordure and blood. The explosion – the *Solon* – had done its terrible work.

There was no sign of Krachter and Mara, but at the far end of the space a huge ramp led up – the remains of a plank trapdoor hanging off its hinges.

The *Solon*, tucked under my arm, was vibrating violently; almost as if sharing the creatures' terror. Suddenly, Tiroc Og was behind us. 'They're on the roof. Follow me!' he screamed, charging past us towards the ramp. Kami darted after him, ropes dangling from both shoulders. I armed my crossbow and followed.

We were back on top of the tor but now on the far side of the walled enclosure opposite the lightning rod, still barely able to stand, battered by the wind and shrouded in an icy cloud mist which smattered my skin like thousands of needles. A huddle of moving figures shifted ahead on the far side of the enclosure just visible in the cloud fog, their forms lit by a shaky firebrand dipping in and out of the mist, among them a scaly wing. More Skarag!

Pushing ourselves into the teeth of the wind we stumbled and slid through the cloud towards the huddle, the *Solon* shuddering at my back, as if echoing my own dread. Momentarily the mist lifted to reveal four of the lizard birds flapping around a flattish, boat-like structure, an open-sided palanquin, their claws clutching each corner, as it hovered a few feet above the surface. Buffeted by the blast they were trying with difficulty to hold it in the air. I saw a flash of blue robe, a struggling figure between two Skraeling. Mara – being dragged on to the shaky palanquin.

I glimpsed Krachter, back to us, facing a tall, hooded figure in white strapped into a chair at the back of the palanquin. Kahl! At his feet sat a fearsome Skraeling, skeletal, insect-eyed, silver haired – but in the ochre robes of a renouncer. Around the Morok leader were more of the dreadful tribe, bristling with armour and weapons, but struggling to stay steady in their focus on getting Mara on board and trying to steady the wildly swaying palanquin. At first, curiously, none of them seemed aware of our proximity. Tiroc Og's night sight concoction still coursing through my body, I could clearly see their shapes, their faces sheathed in a sickly orange glow – an aura of evil – and I saw Mara now on board, lying comatose on the strange platform.

The blind skryer looked straight at me. He, alone it seemed, knew we were there. He calmly pointed his clawed hand at me and I heard his broken voice, commanding even over the howling winds, croaking, 'They're behind you, Krachter. Kill the rebels, if 'tis the last thing ye ever do. But not the young Albin. Bring him and that which he carries on his back. If he wants to see his mother again in her life, he must come with me.'

Krachter spun round, shock and horror on his face and began barking orders. Some of the Skraeling on the palanquin, struggling to stand, clumsily encircled Kahl and Mara. But the rest, about a dozen or more, started falling chaotically to the ground before scrambling to their feet, arming crossbows and raising double-edged axes. Then a thick cloud descended on the scene, obscuring everything.

'Kami, Tiroc Og, get behind me!' I yelled, as we instinctively dropped behind the wall. A shower of darts flew over our heads. 'Stop the firing!' I screamed in Ironese above the uproar, lifting my head inches above the wall. 'I, Osian of Faron, will speak to Kahl. Let me speak!' My words echoed around the space, booming even above the wind.

'Wait,' came a reply from the direction of the palanquin, in a strange, metallic echo, audible over the howling blast. The firing stopped. But we could see nothing – not even where the Skraeling were.

'I am here,' I shouted, dropping my crossbow and reaching for my *papose*, 'I have what you want. I *will* come to you. You must first release Mara, let her go with my friends here and allow them to leave this place in safety. Tell your guards to stand down.'

I held my *papose* in the air. Strangely, the *Solon* didn't resist, but there was a strange noise between my ears, almost like a conch call, coming in waves and getting louder. I walked forward around the walled enclosure into the teeth of the storm and saw two lines of Skraeling between me and the palanquin, their weapons lowered.

Then came a sudden lightning flash. The roof of the tor lit up in a bright orange glow, blowing away the fog, exposing every detail of the awful scene before us. Then a second flash forked upon the lightning rod, sending a stream of fire between us and the palanquin, engorging the nearest of the oncoming Skraeling guards. At this the Skarag took fright. The palanquin lurched away from the edge, the lizard birds beating their snake wings frantically. Kahl rose to his feet and beckoned to me with his bony twisted hand. From the dark sockets of his eyes came an eerie hypnotic purple glow. His broken voice was in my head, audible over the screaming of the burning Skraeling and the roar of the winds. 'Come,' he said. 'Bring it. I will release her. Come to me.' The palanquin was hovering barely a few feet above the roof. The winds were against me, pushing me backwards, but Mara was a few paces away from me. It was possible. I could do it. The *Solon* and me for her.

In a daze I found myself moving towards the palanquin, the *papose* in my hand, quivering like a frightened animal. I heard the muffled voice of my mother, 'No, Osian. No!' But I carried on. Then suddenly from behind I heard the call of Tiroc Og's conch. One, two, three sharp notes. The signal for attack!

The many sounds of the cacophony merged into one – a steady, thrumming drone. Everything fell still: the Skarag fell silent, their wings and the palanquin frozen in space. Kahl and I alone could move, as if the two of us were travellers in a separate dimension, another place and time. He stood, his eye sockets glowing, his outstretched talons gesturing me forward. I felt a short searing pain in my chest, as if something was reaching into it and dragging out my inner being, groping for my soul.

He spoke again. 'Come, Kyron. Bring it. I will release her. Come to me.' Kyron? It wasn't my name, yet something deep inside me recognised it. I muttered the word, 'Kyron,' but it meant nothing. As I approached, the *papose* began to glow, green but pulsing purple like Kahl's eyes. My hands were burning. I was being dragged forward, pain searing through my body. But as the *Solon* pulsed, alternately green and purple, I felt myself being hauled back. My hands turned ice cold, then hot again. I had become the vessel of a struggle between two forces more powerful than anything I could control. One force was with me but the other seemed to want not just the *Solon*, but my soul – to destroy my earthly body.

The drone became louder and louder till I thought my ears were going to burst and then I was being dragged into the palanquin.

Then came another bolt of lightning, a flash of green light enveloping everything. The *papose* glowed bright green, strong like summer leaf. I heard Kahl scream. 'Kyron! You will come... you will come...' but his voice began fading, becoming distant, weakening. The pain in my chest eased.

Then the world returned.

I was standing on the very edge of the tor. The palanquin was bouncing around chaotically, the Skarag struggling in the wind with great, heavy wingbeats. Around me flew volleys of bolts and arrows into the mass of confused Skraeling, sending the last of them tumbling over the edge.

Mara was lying unattended on the floor of the palanquin, somehow loosed from the grip of her captors and sliding towards the void. The palanquin was just out of my reach. I screamed her name.

Suddenly Kami was beside me, shouting. 'Grab this. It'll steady you, then pull on mine when it stops runnin!' as to my amazement he launched himself into the air, his cloak unfolding like the wings of a bird.

Hardly understanding what he meant, I grabbed with my free hand at something he'd pushed at my waist. A rope. It was taut, tied off to something behind me.

I was astonished to see Kami landing upon the wavering palanquin before deftly throwing a loop of rope around my mother, then sliding off with her into the void, loops of rope flying wildly behind, then disappearing from sight.

The palanquin was also gone, into the swirling mist. But I heard a voice echoing in my head. *His* voice. 'What yeh have is mine, Kyron. I *will* come for it. And then yer life with it,' followed by a furious groan. Horrible, demented, unearthly. Then nothing.

I had no time to ponder his threat, for my attention was on Kami's rope, now rubbing on the edge of the tor. Kami and Mara were down there, somewhere, hopefully still tied together. Grabbing the rope, I pulled on it with all my might, backed away and got as far as the enclosure wall where I was able to brace my feet against it. Then others joined me, taking the rope, their muscles straining. Bran, Tiroc Og were there. And faces I couldn't see through the clouds and my tears. 'Pull!' I heard Tiroc Og yelling.

Gradually the rope began to come up. But the winds were worsening again and the rope had come to a stop, fibres snapping on the edge of the tor. The voices of my friends became frantic. I leaned and pulled with all my might, still with one hand on my *papose*.

What happened next took place in a complete blur. I felt a shadow dart beside me, wrenched away the *papose* and bowled me over as from somewhere deep inside me came a screech, like an animal in pain. I'd been knocked to my stomach, the breath forced from me, my body racked with pain. I was weakened, unable to move. But I saw who it was.

Krachter! He had the *Solon*! And I could do nothing. Couldn't even get to my feet. I saw him pushing into the wind along the edge of the tor towards the rope, a long shield on his back, my *papose* with the Solon in his grip. I tried to rise but couldn't.

I saw him pull out a dagger and hold it above the rope. 'Lay down your weapons,' he hissed. 'All of you, or I'll cut it through.'

'Cut it and you die, Krachter,' Tiroc Og shouted back.

'Rebel dogs. Look below!' he screamed back. 'My army of thousands surround the island. Kill me and yeh'll all meet yer death. Abandon yerselves to my mercy, the mercy of Kahl. Look around yeh.' He pointed to the east, where over the lake and beyond the edge of the mountain a clearing in the clouds and the light of dawn had revealed a sea of moving swords, bristling spears and shields that seemed to fill the land all the way to the seaport. To the west, on Krater Lake, a huge flotilla of long boats had already landed; warriors were flowing from them. It seemed we, the tor, the island, were indeed surrounded.

We'd come so far, but in the end it looked hopeless. The rope holding my mother and Kami had stopped running and was fraying, badly, Krachter's eyes darting between it and us. Yet, the loss of the *Solon* had been too much; I felt the life force draining from me.

Then, remembering what Grandfather had said about the strength in breath, inhaling as deeply as I could I managed to find and arm my sling. And with the outbreath I rolled onto my back, pointed it at Krachter and fired.

Amazingly, the shot flew past his shield and hit his arm sending the dagger into space. Stunned, he hesitated before darting to the side, still with my *papose*. The cloud mist had descended again, obscuring my view. Taking another few deep breaths, invigorated by my first strike, I re-loaded and waited. The cloud passed over. I saw him running, breathed in and out and fired again. Again, I struck home – his other arm, this time causing him to drop the *papose* before disappearing somewhere into the cloud mist. It skidded across the floor and somehow, miraculously, was near me. I retrieved it. The pain I'd felt inside dissipated, strength flooding back into my body. Jumping to my feet, I ran to the edge of the tor and clutched at Kami's rope. It was still taut. Somewhere in the fog behind me my friends were valiantly holding on. But it was so badly frayed, only one fibre kept it there. I darted to the edge and reached out into the abyss to get a better hold.

'I'm losing it!' I screamed, clutching the rope below the fraying section. No use. It was ready to break.

Suddenly, Tiroc Og and Bran were by my side, holding me back from falling over the edge. Kami and Mara were a single strand away from crashing to their doom. And I couldn't hold on any longer.

'Use it again, Osian, use yer weapon!' I heard Tiroc Og shout above the blast. I breathed in deeply, closed my eyes and with every last ounce of concentration, *willed* the *Solon* to help.

At first, nothing. Then came the green flash and the world went still. Everything around me, even the winds and shifting cloud mist, were frozen. I felt a wave of vigour and power racing through me. Then the world returned; just as the rope snapped, I fell back, almost tumbling over my helpers.

But in my hand was the rope end holding Kami and Mara. I was able easily to pull it upwards and back over the precipice, hardly aware of the weight at the other end. My friends watched on in amazement as I calmly stood and, as if in a trance, wrapped the rope around my middle then began walking backwards. I felt as if I was in a dream, every movement as easy and smooth as if the burden on the rope was lighter than air.

'I can see 'em,' shouted Bran. He was lying precariously on the edge looking down the tor. 'Keep pullin', Osian, Kami's coming up… Mara too.'

I stood by the walled enclosure, my heart pumping wildly and kept winding it in, the rope piling onto the floor behind me. More shouting. I tied it off at the great metal pinion holding the lightning rod and walked to the edge, still winding it in and looked over: there was Kami, abseiling upwards, bouncing off the sides of the tor, coming closer with every bound, the limp figure of Mara lashed to his chest. Still I wound it in, the rope running through my hands as though it was nothing.

Then they were over the edge. Kami laid the limp form of Mara in my arms, her face ghostly white and no longer breathing. I carried her into the enclosure out of the wind, only vaguely aware of the figures moving around me, creating a circle of protection. For Krachter was still around somewhere and who know who – or what – else.

My lips on hers, I began forcing my breath into her lungs. Again, again. Then, just when I thought it was no use, to my absolute joy, she began to stir, then half-opened her eyes. Seeing me, she smiled. I gave her my flagon and she drank, then I lay back, contented. I was with her at last. Saved. But for how long? What now? I glanced around me as it sunk in just how desperate our situation still was. Had we come all this way only to die together, on a ruinous tower on a remote island surrounded by an enemy horde? And there was nothing our meagre few, even with the *Solon*, could do against that.

My head drooped. I held Mara close as if it were the last time. Then, Tiroc Og's conch again sounded from somewhere behind me, echoing across the wastes, the notes long and deep. Three times it roared. And with each calling the shell in the *papose* at my feet throbbed and pulsed, seeming to amplify the sound of the conch above everything, even the fury of the winds.

Then came the answering, other conches – many of them. And, from the distance, a thunderous banging. Around us debris flew high into the air, like the outpourings of erupting volcanoes, pieces of stone and wood clattering onto the roof of the tor, compounding the chaos of wind and cloud and the confusion of death and life – and the tumult in my chest and heart.

'Look!' yelled Bran excitedly. 'Yeh must look.'

Laying Mara's head on my *papose* I stood up, unsure what to expect. The clouds around the tor had evaporated again. I had a clear view of the island and beyond. Then I realised what had made Bran so animated. The flotillas Krachter had pointed out weren't Morok. The enemy fleet at the far port beyond the mountain was aflame and their black sailed vessels on Krater Lake were sinking or lying on their sides like broken spiders webs. A full-scale battle was raging on the landing sites; everywhere, brightly coloured flags fluttered and snapped. Enemy troopers were fleeing from the port palisades in wild confusion – straight into the worst of incoming cannon fire. Wave upon wave of flaming arrows – Cana-Din, the rebel leader's signature weapon – punctured the skyline, pouring into the heart of their defences. Trapped and terrified, the Morok were rushing hither and thither, those not falling on land diving into Krater Lake, inevitably to drown or meet a terrible end in the claws and teeth of fearsome predators.

Cana-Din and her army: hordes of Brach, Sideag and many other tribes. They'd come after all.

I watched for a moment, my eyes tearing, my chest swelling. A fresh cloud of debris started to fall. I raised my cloak over Mara to protect her from debris, only to catch her awake, sitting up, mouthing a scream and staring in terror at something over my shoulder. I whipped round. Krachter, an armed crossbow in his hands, had emerged from the far stairwell. Bran and Kami, busy looping ropes, had their backs to him. Tiroc Og was nowhere to be seen. I was weaponless.

'Die, Albin!' I heard him yell as a fresh wave of debris tumbled around us. But his deadly missile, crashing into the tumult, tumbled uselessly on to the ground at my feet. Desperately he pulled back the bow string for another attempt.

But the bolt never flew. He'd gone rigid, falling to his knees, blood pouring from his mouth. Then he toppled forward, a burning arrow embedded deep in his back.

Who? A tall figure in a grey cloak carrying a moonsilver longbow stepped out from the stairwell; a vision, it seemed, from another world, a stately She-Eronn, long mane flowing loose across her shoulders down a sungold breastplate to a waist-belt stuffed with knives and arrows. Her face was war painted grey with dark green stripes; her mane the colour of fire ash. Her eyes blazed blue like the sky, just like the apparition in the Marten's fire. But this was no golden princess; this was a warrior unlike anything I ever could imagine. It was the glorious Cana-Din!

Stepping over Krachter as if he was a piece of dirt, she strode onto the roof, barking orders at the green cloaked figures pouring up behind her and came forward. I could think of nothing to say and felt only a strange pummelling in my chest.

With barely a glance at me, she took in the scene on the roof of the tor: Mara on the deck, the dead guards, Kami busily stripping their weapons, his ropes ready piled. Turning to Bran, she asked, 'You. Brach. Was Kahl here?'

The giant Brach bowed at the vision before him. 'He wuz, but got away.'

She frowned, and said, 'Tiroc Og is below with Gwion-Din. I will go back there. My father is in his last hours in this life. Your brave friends Ganoc and Lakon are at the palisades with my warriors, with all your company, who I am to tell you, are well and send their wishes. We are pleased to see you live, friend Brach.' Then, with a curt nod at me and a swish of her mane, she was gone.

Cana-Din. My head reeled; my legs shook. Little wonder she struck terror into the hearts of Morok. The legend. I'd seen her. At last.

13

THE FINAL CALL

Sometime later, in the Moon of the Popping Cherries, following the taking of Rakhaus and the freeing of the slaves, Tiroc Og's company and myself were in Clachoile, the Stone Forest, home to the Brach. We'd been summoned to the great hall of the Bear Fathers, a cavernous chamber carved from the side of a cliff on the edge of Jerumin, in the heart of the forest. We were to be addressed by Amon, High Chief of the Brach and reputedly the greatest orator in all Manau. So, here I stood, friends and family all around, thinking of everything I'd been through and contemplating where my future lay, my thoughts returning again and again to the problem of the *Solon*. And then there was the lovely Gimin, whom I hadn't seen since the fall of Rakhaus.

It was almost impossible to believe, but there'd been no casualties amongst the company, though there were injuries, odd burns and bruises from the debris thrown up when the Tor of Doors and the Bell Tor collapsed. There were deaths among unexperienced warriors of the free tribes as they came face to face with the enemy horde issuing in panic from the burning palisades. But such was the force and surprise of Cana-Din's assault, the Morok presence on Rakhaus and the lands between Fire Mountain and the coast had been wholly demolished. They remained however in control of westernmost Erainn, about half of the territory, licking their wounds encamped in the forests and hills around Erintor. But it was no secret that the great Wester tribes towards the south, the Rhuad, the Rigead and their allies were planning an assault, the only question was when – and whether the Brach and the Sideag would be involved.

I'd seen Bran only once while resting and recuperating in Clachoile and not much of Tiroc Og either. Both were busy dealing with prisoners and the transport of freed slaves to homelands not under Morok control. I was glad to be not involved and able to spend time helping Faron with Mara's recovery.

In this time, I'd seen Gimin only briefly, an exchange of smiles from a distance that sent my chest a-fluttering. I'd heard she'd been alongside Cana-Din during the siege and afterwards had been busy working with the freed slaves accommodated in huge makeshift camps dotted around Clachoile, helping the injured and sick. I feared at first that she'd leave with her Rhuad friend Reyn's fleet back to their homelands. But I was relieved to hear that she was to remain for the time being in Clachoile with the rest of Tiroc Og's original company, though whether I would be able to develop a more intimate friendship in my time remaining here I was unsure – and it troubled me.

I also felt misgivings about leaving the company when there was so much to be done. The Morok had been roundly thumped but not vanquished. Krachter was dead, but Kahl was back in Erintor, licking his wounds and supposedly rebuilding his armoury – that included, so it was said, a terrible weapon that would destroy all.

I'd been room sharing with the wonderful Eronn, Drion, in Amon's stone house where Faron and Mara were recovering and getting ready for our return to Alba. Drion was to return with us.

He had no living family and the itinerant life of Tiroc Og's band of young warriors had diminished appeal. I'd made good friends with him. Despite his disability – he was one armed – he was very skilled in carpentry and stonework. He was also a brilliant cook, of course; and his fishmeal and red berry porridge was the highlight of our mornings in Amon's household. Ten or so summers younger than Faron and Mara, I knew he'd be a good companion to them back home and I imagined him sharing fireside stories with Grandfather – whom, we'd learned from the harriers, was alive and well and anticipating our return.

Kami, with faithful Yamis and his brother, was to go to Alba with us, along with a troop of Amon's fiercest warriors. A confiscated Aguan full sailing vessel was being readied to carry us from the coast and from there to follow the eastern and southern shores of the Great Lake of Rising and Falling Water. This was longer than the north-west passage through the Broken Sea, navigable through the icefields, but too close to Skraelandia – and Skraeling pirates – for comfort. We would take port in Rhegad, friendly Rhuad territory; from there travelling north by wagon and then a mule-drawn sled up through the snow passes of the White Mountains, reaching Alba after three moons. Any enemy boats on the Great Lake would be no match for an Aguan schooner, captained by Kami, fully decked with sails and – I understood – a complete spread of cannon.

Still yet to fully come to terms with my leaving, I glanced around at the grand gathering of warriors, their tribal elders and chiefs at the forefront in the glorious headdresses of their clans, hands resting patiently upon their totem staffs. Brach and the Sideag were the most numerous, but I recognised the headdresses and cloak colours of many other tribes: Beaver, Deer, Horse, Grey Cat, White Wolf, Fox, Red Wolf, Crow and Hawk. Eronn, so depleted in numbers, were few, but were there, along with representatives of the smaller surviving Erainn tribes. There were no Marten or Wind Hare, and only Kami was here to represent the Tarsin. He was swaddled in ropes as usual, standing on the far side of Faron and Drion. I stood alongside proud Yamis and the incredible Ganoc, the rest of Tiroc Og's company around us. The hall glowed in the light of a great roaring fire.

No sign of Gimin. Or of the glorious Cana-Din, or her fearsome dark green cloaked and masked followers.

After some time of waiting, Chief Amon, in a headdress of black bearskin braided with eagle feathers, entered to a fanfare of conches, followed by Bran, splendidly dressed in a long cloak of bearskin decked with jet and silver necklaces, but looking embarrassed. Now apparently reconciled with Amon, his father, he had become the heir designate, though, he'd told me, Amon, despite his great age, had no plan to relinquish leadership of the greatest of the free tribes. Bron, his younger brother by one *hora* followed, then various Brach princesses, their great stature augmented by the natural beauty of their faces and the high colour of their ceremonial dress.

On the wall behind them hung an array of cruel black Morok weaponry and other souvenirs of the battle: Ferok robes; Krachter's bloodied mail shirt; recovered stolen jewellery and fine-spun cloth; and in prominent position, the red robe taken from Morc by Tiroc Og when he'd killed the Wildcat traitor and used it to gain access to the Tor of Winds.

Amon walked up to a stone dais carved into the shape of a giant bear, bowed to it then turned and bowed to the assembly. Bron took up position to his right, Bran to his left. Alongside them stood Reyn, remarkable in a headdress of swan feathers, representing his father, High Chief of the Rhuad, as well as the chiefs of the Rideag, the Red Wolf and the other tribes of the 'sunset' lands. There too was the formidable Arca, High King of the Sideag, a giant timber wolf's head draped over a cloak of furs and eagle feathers, a forked hazel staff in his right hand with a bright blue stone glistening in the crook. Thus were the four most powerful of the free tribes of Greater Manau: the

Rhuad, the Rigead, the Brach and the Sideag, represented together in one place.

Mara was still weak but recovering well, being tended by Amon's personal shaman. Faron and I were the only two present from the Albin tribe. In my *papose* nestled the *Solon*, wholly quiescent since the liberation of Rakhaus. Only Tiroc Og, Bran and Kami had seen its outer form with the mark of the Morok and knew of what it was capable. My friends in Tiroc Og's band had certainly seen its power. No-one, including me, had seen whatever was inside the shell, or knew what it was. Tiroc Og, I was certain, knew more than he was prepared to reveal, other than what he had already indicated.

I'd already heard in detail of the fortunes of our friends after we'd left them when we entered Elvintal from below. Apparently, on hearing echoes of the thunderstick explosions, they left the tunnel and followed Bran's trail of tiny god-stones. Masked against the smoke, they were able to circle the Tor of Doors relatively unchallenged and pass the Bell Tor just before it collapsed. Then, entering the Tor of Winds through a hole blown in the side by thundersticks, they'd swiftly dealt with any Morok that remained inside – for most had fled or tried to flee into the palisades and beyond.

The involvement of the free tribes in the storming of Rakhaus had been very much touch and go right up to the moon in which it took place. In the end, Amon and Arca lent their considerable weight to the endeavour on learning that Cana-Din had secured the full commitment of the western tribes. A red-sailed fleet containing an army of the Rhuad and their allies were already ready and waiting off the Aguan coast for the signal to move in. Not to be outdone by their former rivals, the Brach and the Sideag had no choice but to commit and once in, they threw everything and everyone at it.

The final piece in the jigsaw, perhaps the one single event that turned the tide in the favour of the allies, was the sudden withdrawal of the supplies, munitions and warriors promised to Kahl by Iskar,

King of the Red Skraeling, even to the extent of abandoning Kahl's Skraeling guards to their fates (all killed, except for the strange priest I'd seen escaping with Kahl).

The Skraeling fleet stationed offshore had moved back to allow the Rhuad ships to sail in; and the Skraeling army billeted at the Rakhaus ports simply stood by as the slaughter of the Morok commenced. Iskar's treachery, I'd been told, came about after a visit from a special envoy dispatched to Skraelandia by Cana-Din. What had been promised to the Skraeling King in return was a fact unshared, and like the identity of the envoy, remained a closely guarded secret.

On that fateful day the gods and the Fates were on our side – Tiroc Og's surviving harrier had escaped the clutches of Krachter's eagle and had let Cana-Din know we were about to venture into the tunnel. Half the enemy army had become ensnared in Rakhaus's western marshes (thanks to Tiroc Og's deliberate misinformation) and the other half sheltering within wooden palisades were easy picking for Cana-Din's flaming arrows, the fortifications becoming walls of fire. Engulfed and surrounded in flames, trapped and terrified, those Morok that escaped were easily picked off by the free tribes. No quarter was shown even to the wounded. Thousands died but camp followers, females, old and young, were spared and interned. Of those that managed to return from the marshes, few survived and escapees into the lake did not live long. Such were their destinies. As they had lived, so they died.

As to how I got to this place – alive – many, many questions remained unanswered, some of them still unsettling: the whole tragic business with Romi; Garidh's double cross; my other narrow escapes. Then there was the sensation of being watched – followed, even – the moment I stepped foot into the Erainn borderlands; never mind finding and becoming sort of possessed by the *Solon*. 'Why me?' I muttered, my mind drifting about everywhere like wind driven wavelets on a pool instead of on the majestic spectacle before my eyes.

There were other puzzles too: the weird tale of the Marten and how I was somehow connected to it, the vision of Erin in the fire, those eyes, and Tiroc Og's strange observations about prior connections between my family and the *Solon* and between us and Kahl himself.

I snapped to, just as Amon began to speak, holding high in his hands a stave that glittered sungold in the firelight as he spoke, his voice sonorous, commanding, his words echoing around the hall.

'Brothers, sisters, honoured guests. Just as the great sun wheels around the sky, our tribes have returned again as friends. Many moons have passed since the end of the Marsh Wars. Deep is the sword we have buried between ourselves and the Eronn. Terrible lessons have been learned and it is a sadness to me that the pride of the Eronn has been brought so low by the devils that took their sacred homelands – and are still present there. We, the Brach, also have been humbled, weakened by the Long Winter and shamed into action by the bravery and actions of our rebel friends. And we have learned much. In this new time of swords, held no longer at one another, but at the throats of a common enemy, it is a time also when great wisdom is needed.'

Murmurings of assent came from the crowd. Amon again held up his stave – the ancient talking stick of the Chiefs of the Brach – and continued in a lowered voice redolent with sadness. 'I am long in summers. Too long. When the Morok first crossed the Great Lake of Rising and Falling Water my tribe was weak with the Long Winter, so I chose the path of peace over the way of war. We, the Brach,' here he hesitated, 'may have our differences with the Eronn, and the holy lands of Erainn are not in our charge, but the pilgrim ways that run through it must be freed and thereafter open to all. Erainn's anointed guardians were at fault for submitting to Kahl's subterfuge and have paid for it with the lives of their loved ones. But as long as Kahl's devils remain in Manau, controlling the Erainn heartlands, obstructing the old ways, their continued presence is a threat to all who value their freedom – and an offence to the gods.'

Again, murmurings of agreement echoed round the hall from the assembly. Amon paused, lifted again the stave and started again, this time his voice louder. 'The gods we know are angry. The dark clouds that hid the sun and the storms that shook our earth and flooded our fields forged an easy trail for the imposter. We, as mere mortals, cannot draw down the path of the sun; we cannot banish the clouds to warm our fields and homes once again, but if we are to appease the gods and the *sidhe*, our great mothers and fathers, we must show them that we can put our own halls in order, seek their help and pray that they will favour us in return.'

This sentiment was commended with much rattling of totem sticks and murmurs of 'Yahl save us.'

'Rakhaus,' he continued in a manner more measured, 'was a mighty victory. Our brothers and sisters freed; Morok workcamps destroyed; the plumes from the outlanders' burning bodies darker and more foul smelling than the stink of any fumes from Fire Mountain. Any that escaped by boat are scattered across the Broken Sea, easy prey for the sharks and pirates. They are of little use to Kahl, for such is his nature, he will let those that failed him rot till domesday.'

'Meantime the pretender's army dwells yet in the forests at Erintor, around the ancient halls of the Marcher Lords in more terrible slave camps. The pilgrim ways, the shrine of the God of the Wood, the path to our burial grounds, remain forbidden to us. And, I have come at last to understand, as long as we cannot honour the *sidhe*, cannot worship our gods through pilgrimage, cannot make offerings to the shrine, so the Long Winter will remain with us.'

At this there were loud gasps, as some will not have made the connection between the Long Winter and Kahl's presence in Erainn offering succour from it.

Amon raised his staff, then after a pause he continued, the tone firm, assertive. 'We must decide how next to act. It is for this we are gathered here today. I must obtain your counsel; the advice of all the free tribes, friends, new friends and old foes alike.' He looked around the hall. 'But before we talk further, I will ask the son of Lir Og to speak.'

Totem staves were rattled on the ground as a sign of respect for my friend and his remarkable achievements. On this occasion, draped in ceremonial dress, his totem stave resplendent with cat skulls and fresh white eagle feathers, Tiroc Og walked forward, bowed, accepted the silver stave from Amon and turned to face the assembly. The green stone at his wrist sparkled in the firelight, and his yellow mane – losing none of its lustre during the hazard filled course of our adventure – glimmered softly.

'Great Chief of the Brach, chiefs, fathers, and mothers of the free tribes, I greet yeh. I and my brothers in arms are indebted to yeh all – our lives are yers.'

Cheering followed, then he talked briefly of our journey to Rakhaus leading up to a discourse of what he had learned of the Morok and their ways. To most of us it was familiar stuff. Notably, he did not express any theories on the origins of the Morok; nor on what had and was still motivating Kahl. He didn't of course talk about me or the *Solon*. But as he spoke, his audience listening in rapt silence, I became aware of a pair of eyes drilling into me among a group of figures standing at one side of the hall. I turned my head and saw a tall figure in an ochre robe – the garb of mendicants, face deep in his hood, a flicker of firelight revealing a white bearded chin. The figure beckoned to me, raised a staff and signalled. *We should talk.* Whoever it was, was male, aged – and not Eronn. I looked at his stave. It was green, with a bright blue stone at the head. I nodded and he signalled back: *later*. Then he was gone, disappearing into the crowd behind him.

Tiroc Og was still speaking. 'Brave Cana-Din,' he said, 'cannot be with us. She,' he said with a tremor in his throat, 'attends the great Gwion-Din as he prepares for his journey to the land of the *sidhe*.' He paused, then recounted to the assembly how the victory at Rakhaus had come about through the intervention of the great Eronn Elder's daughter. He extolled her for keeping alive the spirit of the free tribes during the darkest moons of the Morok's ascending path of conquest, when so many others had abandoned their fates to the invaders.

Strangely, as he talked of her, there came again to my mind the vision in the fire at the Marten's cabin. Those eyes had blazed out at me. They were Cana-Din's eyes, Erin's proud defiant spirit come to life in the terrible beauty of the bandit queen. I had to repay the life-debt I now owed her. Were it not for her, Krachter's bolt would have struck home. So, I knew I'd see those eyes again, somehow, somewhere, for that debt to be settled.

Then I thought of that other life debt. To Gimin. She hadn't joined the renegades grouped around me, nor could be seen among the Rhuad or Cana-Din's warrior band on the other side of the hall. While the prospect of seeing Cana-Din again was just downright scary, unsettling, not being able to be with Gimin, to talk freely with her like a friend – or more – was eating at me. Earlier when I'd enquired of her, no-one seemed to know where she was at that precise moment, never mind what her intentions were. And I was soon to set off for Alba with my kin.

Was I simply meant to seek her out, keep enquiring until I tracked her down? But to what end? My interest in her was crazy, in a way. We'd barely ever talked and had spent very little time together on the journey. We were virtual strangers from different and distant tribes, yet the way she looked at me I felt as if we'd known each other for ever. There was a bond between us, unspoken, in the eyes and the guts; my entrails already entwined with hers. I wondered too if she was avoiding me – eluding involvement in an impossible situation?

To distract myself I tried to think of being home, of the comforts of our peaceful lakeside dwelling: the whisper of the wind in the eaves, the call of water birds through my little window, and being reunited with Grandfather, still my greatest friend upon this earth. Tiroc Og's surviving harrier had visited and returned with news that Annan was well, and well cared for by my father's sister. I could almost smell her cooking, and how welcome that would be after a moon of standard Clachoile fare: dried forest fungi, soups of frog and tree bark, dried berries and pulses, slugs in fermented goatmilk with the occasional dried beef stew or roasted small game preserved in salt. Here in Clachoile, Drion's porridge was a lifesaver!

All the same, whether it was new calls on my heart, or a result of the changes that had taken place in me, or both, the prospect of going home, now that it was imminent, had lost some of its lustre. I was also acutely aware of my unfinished business. Was it right for me to leave Tiroc Og and our sisters and brothers in arms to carry on the fight to finish what we'd started, banish the Morok and free Erainn? Then there was the question of the *Solon*. It had been fully quiescent since the arrival in Clachoile. Was I just meant to take it home with me? Then what?

I'd caught Faron and Mara stealing occasional wary glances at my *papose*. How much they knew I had no idea, but they'd become aware, or been made aware, of extraordinary things happening around me. They'll have seen me keeping the *papose* close, almost furtively. But they did not query it.

More importantly, I needed advice on what I had to do to separate myself from the *Solon* – if I could. I'd not had the chance of any discussion with Tiroc Og and we were a mere few days away from our departure. There was also another mystery that needed clearing up. Krachter addressed me as "Kyron", a name I'd never heard before, yet it was somehow familiar. What in Yahl's name was that all about?

Up at the top of the hall, Tiroc Og was winding up, his voice raised as he cast his eyes around the mighty assembly. 'Chiefs, brothers, the Morok are not defeated, merely licking their filthy wounds. We must be relentless in our mission, *not* give them time to recover. Join us then, with the wind at our backs, to drive Kahl and his devil hordes from Erainn – and, if we can, from all of Manau.'

Again, this was followed by much cheering and rattling of staves. 'Meantime,' he continued, 'Cana-Din and our brothers and sisters in arms will continue the fight – with or without anyone else at our shoulders. But...' he paused, 'we of the renegade parties are few and the odds against us are overwhelming. Without the might of *all* the free tribes, we'll more and likely die in the endeavour, but at least the great *sidhe* and those that follow, if any, will know we *tried*.'

Then, turning to face Amon, he said, 'I am grateful to yeh, Great Chief, to hear the wisdom of yer years. However, yer brave tribe choose to go forward, 'tis my hope that at least ye'll allow Bran, Bron and Hakon of the Brach to remain by my side. That is what I, son of Lir Og, have to say, Yahl save us all.'

With a flourish he bowed and returned the talking stick. Amon took it back and said, 'The cub of my brother has spoken with wisdom beyond his winters. If we are to win back the favour of the gods, we must drive the Morok beyond all our borders. I speak only for the Brach, but we consent to support our brave friends in their great struggle. However,' he added, raising his voice, 'if we are to win, we cannot fight alone. So, I say join Tiroc Og and Cana-Din, join us. That is what I, Amon of Brannic, Chief of the Brach, have to say.'

He sat down to a tumult of cheering. Then came a sudden silence, a moment of suspense as the mighty Arca, High Chief of the Sideag, the great Grey Wolf, stood up and held out a hand for the talking stick. 'Great Chief Amon, friends, brothers, sisters,' he said, frowning as he spoke. 'There are no Morok in the lands of the Sideag. There are no funeral grounds in Erainn for my tribe to fight for. We bury our dead among the stones of the forest.'

A muttering grew up from the Sideag present, as fearsome looking a bunch of warriors as I'd seen on my journey, apart from the Red Skraeling, alike them only in that they were lean and drawn in face.

Hunters of wild game, their forests offered meagre pickings in the Long Winter and more war might mean more privations, yet I could tell he and his followers in the hall were unhappy about something. Then we learned what it was.

'Iskar,' Arca continued, 'may have coiled himself round a dead tree like a snake in winter but could uncoil at any moment and once again do Kahl's bidding should he, like the Aguan, deem the rewards greater. 'Tis my fear that more war against the Morok and Skraeling would take my children into starvation. That is what I, Arca of Breca of the Sideag, have to say.'

Some Sideag present were nodding their heads. Tiroc Og looked grim and quickly took back the talking stick.

'Great chief of the Sideag,' he said. 'Noble Arca, yeh say yer sons and daughters are hungry now. But Kahl will seek his revenge on the Sideag, as with all the tribes, for what we have done at Fire Mountain. He'll not stop 'till he takes all the food from the mouths of the children of Arca and swallow it along with the lands of all the tribes: yers, the Brach and even the Rhuad. He seeks mastery of all. His revenge will not be complete till all Manau is under his talons and our lands have been turned to desert.'

Then, raising the stick to quieten the cheering from many, he added, 'Brothers, sisters, chiefs, elders, let yer ears carry back to yer homes hearth fires the news we have learned – from sources with clear minds and true hearts – that Kahl has been building a weapon of mass destruction. If he is able to complete it, to assemble the final parts he seeks, this weapon will have the power of one hundred volcanoes, enough force to challenge the gods themselves. If he succeeds, he will have acquired the very power of a god.'

I heard a collective gasp, of disbelief, of shock; and some mutterings of 'What proof?' and 'Says who?' Tiroc Og paused and glanced around, waiting maybe for someone to query what he'd said. But no-one spoke. If there was doubt in some minds, none were willing to openly gainsay him – to speak out against the great hero of Trisuldur and Rakhaus.

So, he continued. "'Tis our belief that the pretender is searching for some mystery object, that will alone help him complete his weapon, to finish what he started. Until he has it, there is time for us to act. But act we must. As night follows day, there will be a reckoning. Kahl's vengeance will know no bounds. It is our duty to stop him, destroy him before he destroys us. That is what I, Tiroc of Lir Og of the Catton, have to say.'

A terrible idea came to me. The mystery object, the *sidhir*, housed within the black seal in my *papose* that I'd named the *Solon*. Was it this what Kahl wanted to complete his weapon? We knew it was powerful. Maybe it had a potential for evil use – in the wrong hands. It knew this – and didn't want it. It gave me an explanation for why he was so desperate to get hold of it. But my resolve to keep it from Kahl's deadly reach was renewed. For as long as I had breath in my body, he would not get it. But what did this mean to me and my plans? He'd come for me wherever I went. How could I possibly go home and risk the lives of my kin once again?

Arca took up the stick again. 'My brave brother speaks well. His deeds, like that of his father, greatest of the Wildcat chiefs, will be sung at campfires for countless summers to come. We too have heard about this weapon – from some that escaped the slave camps at Erintor. But like so many of the stories that come to our ears, it could be a Morok falsehood, meant to frighten us like the deer of the forest fleeing from a hunting party – straight into a hidden trap. Who, after all, could build such a thing – and where? Would Yahl allow a mere mortal to destroy his world?'

'Yes, the Morok leader has been burned; but is it likely, I ask you, that he risks his own miserable life and what he has salvaged by waging yet another war? As fer the shrines, their loss arises from the sins of the old Erainn Marcher Lords that invoked the anger of the gods. The old curse on that line may well bring him down in the end. Erainn meantime is *lost*. The Eronn are few and far between, scattered across the earth. But the ears and eyes of the Sideag have hearts. There will always be a welcome in our hearth fires for our brother Eronn. They have many skills to teach us. As fer the storms, they like great winter itself, will pass in time; fer my sages tell me this has happened before. The sun will return to warm the earth. Many moons may pass but our forests will fill again with game, enough to warm our bellies and feed our offspring.'

There were voices of assent among the crowd. Arca had a smooth tongue and his message was strong. Even I was almost convinced by it. *Almost*. But my friends looked shocked. Ganoc angrily banged a stick on the ground. However, Bran, standing behind Amon, showed no outward emotion and I saw him exchanging glances with Tiroc Og.

To my surprise, Tiroc Og didn't reach for the stick. Arca looked over at him and said, 'However, brother Catton, be assured, my clan elders and those of our Red cousins in the west will meet and consider the matter further. I, Arca, Chief of the Sideag, have spoken.'

Tiroc Og bowed. Arca handed the stick to Amon who turned it upside down. The assembly was over. Despite Arca's speech, a door remained open. And I wondered if there was a strategy of some kind in it.

Some of those gathered had drifted off, but most stayed, forming small groups. Much discussion followed, with voices heated and loud. I thought of how Kahl had come to power; how he'd tricked the Eronn. Surely a chief with the legendary sagacity of Arca wouldn't allow himself to be tricked? Had something happened, some event of which I was unaware, that had shaped the Sideag chief's response? Why else would he encourage us to allow Kahl and his army to stay at Erintor, still in occupation of holy Erainn and building some terrible weapon? It didn't make sense. And so, I did not believe it.

Bran waved to me and came over to take me for supper, showing no surprise at how the assembly had ended. If my instincts were right, Amon and Tiroc Og had known in advance what the Sideag chief would say and it was part of some design agreed among the chiefs that was being played out – for the ears of the loose-tongued – as Kahl's spies were said to be everywhere. Arca's speech was then just a pantomime, meant to wrong foot Kahl into thinking that the tribes were not united – and would not, without the involvement of all, dare come after him.

Tiroc Og joined us, his face expressionless. 'Osian, my friend. Yeh can rejoin yer kin for victuals later. I'd like yeh to come meet an old friend.'

14

AEHMIR

Intrigued, I followed Bran and Tiroc Og back into the narrow winding stone-carved streets of Jerumin. They walked ahead, deep in conversation, leaving me to my thoughts as I contemplated the remarkable twists and turns of my journey to this remarkable place; my mind returning again and again to a pair of blue eyes shining like azure gems, deep within a bright red flame. And to Gimin, her glorious red mane falling around her shoulders.

The tall stone structures of Jerumin spread over us like the branches of the trees that they'd once been, a forest of stone adapted by Brach and Barod masons from the petrified relics of an ancient volcanic eruption, then softened by the weathering of ice and sun. Since I'd been here, I'd been welcomed across many a threshold, the dwellers affording a hospitality greater than I felt I deserved. For, were it not for one of theirs, Bran of Amon, I wouldn't be alive and able to wander open-eyed through their remarkable streets.

After a while we stopped at a small beehive-like dwelling with a round wooden door set apart from the others. 'Go in, brother,' Tiroc Og said, ushering me forwards. 'We'll find yeh later.'

Crossing the threshold, I entered a circular room with a fire in the centre. An iron tripod stood over the blaze and from it hung a black pot steaming with a herbal infusion that reminded me of summer hay meadows back home. In the half-shadows beyond was a rocking chair, bowing gently fro and to. On it was seated the figure in ochre robes who'd signalled to me at the assembly, calmly smoking a long thin pipe. From a tangle of white hair flowing around a high forehead and set back over a pair of large-long ears shone a pair of bright green eyes. A matching green staff with a blue stone at its head lay across his knees, at his side a long thin silver sword that flashed blue and red in the firelight.

'Osian, son of Faron, of Annan,' he said, rocking his chair gently. 'I am Aehmir.'

The breath caught in my throat. I bowed, face to face at long last with he of the Lepoch, the holy tribe of the Wind Hare, who'd taught Tiroc Og everything he knew. I'd long established in my mind a picture of this venerable figure, whose words I'd carried with me like talismans. I'd imagined him to be severe, partly locked in a world of silent prayer and meditation. But here was a lively, gentle presence – open-heartedness detectable in a gentle reassuring voice. And the *Solon* felt it too. The very moment I entered the chamber I felt a soft purring coming from inside my *papose*.

He pointed me to a stool opposite, then turned and stared into the fire. I sat and waited for him to speak, gazing at the coals, noticing how its multicoloured charcoals glowed like the Marten's fire at the beginning of my journey. A tale-tellers fire. Indeed, on the hearth lay a small thin story stick, half covered by an Eronn cloth, an edge of intricate carvings just visible. Aehmir was a tale-teller!

After a while, he broke the quiet. 'Of course, I knew your grandfather...'

Also, a tale-teller! Aehmir figured in some of his stories. I looked up, almost expecting *"If all were told."* But he paused, as from a side door in swept a glorious She-Brach, long black mane falling to her waist, bearing a plate of small berry cakes. Smiling and bowing to Aehmir, she picked up a ladle, filled two stone cups from the infusion in the pot, set the plate and a stone cup on a carved rock table before me and stood back. She then hovered, beaming at me, until the sage, laughter in his voice, dismissed her with 'Away, hussy.' Whereupon with a sweep of her mane, she glided to the doorway, glanced back at me and left the room, half closing the door behind her. I heard her giggle through the opening, joined by a murmur of other female voices that soon faded away.

I sipped the *tai*, waiting for the sage to speak. He'd removed his hood, revealing a friendly face that I'd heard had seen hundreds of winters but yet was oddly youthful. I'd never seen any of his tribe before, only knew of them by legend. He was tall like Reyn, but wiry. The hands resting gently upon his stave were not those of an aged one. His eyes were his most outstanding feature. They twinkled like the stone on the stave resting against his knees.

'You'll have questions, young Osian,' he said, refilling his pipe and looking expectantly.

'So many, sir, that I don't quite know where to start.'

'I'll answer those I can. But first, I hear you're planning to return to Alba – to the hearth fire of your grandfather – my great friend, Annan. Is this the case?'

'Yes. It is so arranged. Grandfather talked much of you. Gave me your little book of your words, which I bear with me.'

'Yes. We were good friends – still are.'

'You talk as though you have seen him,' I queried, keen to hear any fresh news he might have.

'Yes. I have seen him. He is well. And asks for you. He is pleased for you – what you've done; what you've become. And…' he paused. 'He has a message for you.' There was something odd in the way the sage said this, a hesitation, that he was about to tell me something I might not want to hear.

'Is it about coming home? For I shall be seeing him soon?'

'No. He said that you must fulfil your destiny, your *almadh*. That you must finish what h…s… has been started…'

'What do you mean, sir?' I was sure he was about to say "*he* started" but corrected himself. His accent was unusual to me, his voice both wispy like the wind, yet strong like gusts in the trees – and not every word was clear. I'd misheard this – after all, what on earth could Grandfather have anything to do with all this?

'What I – he – means, young warrior, is that your mission is not complete.'

'But I've achieved what I set out to do. I must now see my kin safely home.'

Aehmir nodded and lifted his pipe to his mouth, relit it, blew out some smoke, then gently rocked back and forward. I looked at the fire, watching the changes in the coals, a turbulence of colour and small smoky forms. But deep within them a darkness seemed to be gathering. I felt a tremor – not of fear exactly, but a disturbance in my mind of that sort; again, I thought of the Marten's fire, how it had changed from light to dark as the tale-teller's story turned ominous.

He leaned over and poked the fire with a stick, rattling the coals till they sparkled bright, and spoke again. 'But things have changed. You cannot go home. It will put all near you in grave danger and would put Annan's life in extreme peril. It is you Kahl seeks. You don't want to be near your family when he finds you – as find you he will.'

'I have become a warrior. I can protect them.'

He just shook his head. Taken aback, I queried, 'Anyway, what am I to such as Kahl?' But I already knew the answer. I squirmed on my seat, staring at the fire, a sudden fresh smoky darkness dampening the flames. And I shivered.

'Kahl is vengeful. And he *must* have that which you carry.' He waved his pipe at my *papose*, now nestled at my feet. Of course, he knew. Tiroc Og will have told him. 'My ears have been ringing,' he continued, 'with the boasts of your warrior friends talking of their accomplishments. But whenever your name is mentioned, the voices go strangely silent. There is wariness – fear, even, in the bravest of all, because of what you bear – they view it as sorcerous.'

'What I bear – the thing that has come to me. I call it the *Solon*.'

'Ah. 'Tis a good name. Tiroc Og told me,' he responded, pausing to relight his pipe and throw fresh kindling on the fire. 'A good name indeed,' he repeated in a mutter, then, raising his head, he looked directly into my eyes. 'You have the name in it. So, it is then yours?'

'I've never thought it was mine,' I replied, 'more I felt as if *I* belonged to *it*. When I tried to let it go, I somehow was prevented from doing so. Yet I know my life will not be fully mine again 'til I separate myself from it, but I know not how. It also has my life in it – and perhaps those of my friends.'

He dragged upon his pipe, sending the smoke up into the ceiling. 'I mean to help you if I can, Osian of Faron. But I have some questions.'

'What can I tell you, that you do not already know?'

I made a gesture to the *papose*, lying at my feet, about to open the drawstrings and produce the *Solon*, seemingly able without having on this occasion to overcome my normal reluctance. But Aehmir started quickly, reached over, touched my arm, shook his head and said firmly, 'Osian, I do not need to see. Tirog Og has *seen* it. It is enough.'

A little startled, I let go the drawstrings and raised my head. In Aehmir's eyes and voice there was no discomfort, no fear of it, almost as if he *knew* it.

'Tell me how it came by you,' he said, 'and everything concerning it since.'

With relief, I told the sage about my journey, how I'd first seen the *Solon* in the cavern, how I'd been drawn to retrieve it from the river, the strange effect it had on me, its mysterious interventions, everything that had happened to me, those I'd met since, leaving no-one and nothing out, as far as I could remember. Aehmir sat silently sipping tea, occasionally smoking and rocking while I talked, every now and then nodding. I saw him stiffen when I came to the Marten's tale, looking pained when I started to tell it, before he cut me off, muttering, 'I know this.' Nothing else evoked any response, even Romi's treachery. Then, when I reached the part where we parted with most of our company at the tunnel before entering Elvintal, he held up his hand. 'Enough. Little need to tell me more. My head reels with the warrior's accounts, though all differ in the details,' he added with smile. 'I must give thanks for your tale – and well told it was. Now you deserve some answers. I will tell you what I can – that is, what I can within my power.'

He put down his pipe and lifted his story stick from the fire side, unfolding the cloth and fingering the carvings. I half expected a story and "*If all were told.*" It was the way he said it, like a tale-teller. But I wanted explanations, truths, not stories.

'You know, young Albin,' he said, 'the coming of Kahl had to do with the curse upon the tribe, unleashed by the fall of the House of Eronn.'

'Yes, Tiroc Og suggested as such.'

'And that the Long Winter has its storm-given roots in those times?'

'Yes,' I replied, reminded of a detail in the Marten's tale, still vivid in my head, that there was an Aehmir in that. The doomsayer. A long-living member of the Wind Hare. Was this him – the same, who'd become a holy man, a wanderer?

As if reading my thoughts, he stiffened and looked away with a light nod of his head. This was my answer. After a brief pause, he said, 'Tell me what happened; how you felt when you saw Kahl for the first time.'

I described the encounter in the courtyard; the sinister sensation of being penetrated by the Morok leader's unseeing eyes.

Aehmir nodded. 'He's a skryer, you know, part-prophet, part-shaman; a creature of the darkness with hidden powers – dangerous powers. He'll have had you in his sights from the beginning of your journey; tracked you in ways known only to the sorcerers. No-one, apart from the gods, can *see* everything, but he can *see* some things. He knows that you have what he wants, young Osian. He'll destroy anything or anyone in his way to get it. But for some reason, in seeking your *Solon*, as you call it, he needs you with it – alive. Were that not so, you'd already be dead.'

I felt a chill run through me. Romi in her confession had also suggested this.

'Do you know, Aehmir, what it is? It behaves like a thing alive, but yet it does not live, move or breathe within the world we live. Whether it was animate before it was sealed, I do not know and have no way of knowing as the seal, it seems, cannot be broken – and I am certain that it is not to be broken. It has been called a *sidhir* by some, a thing of sorcery. But I do not think it is a thing of evil, of malice. It is separate from me, of course, yet it talks through me, though it is still me that is talking, as if I am one with it.'

His lips pursed and under his breath, he mouthed a strange sound: "*Q'aa…*"

I remembered. This my Grandfather once told me was the sound of the Cosmic Tree when shaken by the winds of heaven, when the ravens take to the air and the three golden-eyed Norns, the Fates, cease their constant watering and bow to the ground before Yahl, the *One*, who speaks through the tree.

What, I wondered, could this possibly mean?

191

Aehmir remained silent, his face towards the fire, yet I knew he was not looking into the flames. Then he stirred. For a moment I thought he *was* going to tell a tale. But no. He put down the tale-telling stick, carefully folding it back into its cloth, relit his pipe and said, ''Tis alive, Osian, not in the ways we think – but some other way I cannot explain. And yes, while it is in your care you are indeed possessed by it – but not so that you've lost your will. It is an extraordinary thing… extraordinary in so many ways.

'Why do you think Kahl needs it so badly and – as you tell – me with it?'

'He wants its power – for the things you've yourself seen; maybe for this terrible weapon he's rumoured to be building. As for its *true* nature and purpose, I only know what I understand to be around it – a Xthonic shell woven by an earth dragon; a shell that cannot be broken. That which lies within has an *almadh*, its own destiny. And for some reason, that destiny is entangled with yours.'

'He called me something – up on the Tor; a name I did not know, yet somehow, I did: "Kyron." Who's Kyron? What did he mean by calling me this?'

'You know Askrit, surely.'

I shrugged. None the wiser.

'It is not really a name, but a very old Askrit word for "messenger", rarely used now.'

'Messenger? Meaning?'

He shrugged and stroked his chin. 'That's as much as I can tell you, Osian. It could be taken so many ways.'

Another riddle.

'You speak of shared destinies. But I didn't ask for this, Aehmir. Can I not now be released. Why can't I just return the *Solon* to the river, where I found it?'

He recoiled. 'Yahl forbid! Even if it let you, which I doubt, whoever finds it, should they live long, will be sought out by Kahl, maybe even

Iskar of the Red Skraeling, who now knows of its existence, its power and who has it. And there will be other sorcerers who know of it and might even be seeking it. Kahl certainly believes it is his. He it was who sent those Krol to the earth dragon to seal it. Though how he came to acquire it in the first place is a mystery.'

'Why was it sealed, do you think?'

'It'll be lethal in its raw state. The xthonic flux – the dark webbing of the earth dragon – is poisonous in its raw state. But not when hardened like stone. It was maybe exposure to your *Solon* that made those Krol ill as you have described – and the flux brought them even closer to their ends. They were doomed before they entered that cavern.'

'Is it a danger to me – even sheathed?'

'You are only here – alive – because of it.'

'It is a life debt I have to it, then?' Suddenly I felt trapped. A wave of despondency crept over me. Am I ever to be the way I once was? 'What then am I to do with it, Aehmir? How am I ever to separate myself from it?'

'The answer is obvious, young Albin. You need to return it to its owner, its rightful owner. Only then can you – and maybe even it – have the peace you seek.'

'You think that might be Kahl – that he had it and lost it. He said it was his.'

'Nay, nay. He's not the rightful owner. From what you tell me, it fears him, fears his Morok. As for who the rightful owner is, only the *Solon* itself can guide you.'

'You mean just walk out that door there and go any old where, hoping that someday it will lead me to its owner?' I queried, but immediately dropped my head. In my frustration I was being disrespectful to an elder – a holy one. But Aehmir just stroked his chin and said solemnly, 'There will come a time – and a place.'

'Meantime, what do I do? You said I could not go home.'

'There is a place where you must go. It is far from here, a great journey. But I have to say that of those who go, few return. In fact, I've heard tell of only one,' he said and paused.

I'd already sensed it. 'Kahl,' I blurted.

He nodded.

'What is this place – how do I get there?'

'It lies in the norther parts, across the Broken Sea and beyond the far Krakos Mountains. It's a journey from here of many leagues, of hundreds of moons, even more. The place is a mountain, Kalas, the cosmic centre of the world, around which everything spins including the sun, the moon and all animate and inanimate beings. Atop that mountain is a sacred well, beside it is *Mundi*, the World Tree. And there you must seek guidance.'

'By what means? Prayer?' I asked, half in jest.

Aehmir laughed. 'Well, that's one way, certainly,' he replied with a shrug. 'We can all but seek the wisdom of the gods.'

'You mean I have to figure it out – like a riddle?'

'I suppose a riddle it is, a puzzle that you must solve. Maybe something will be clear when you get there. I can only tell you of the place.'

'How d'you know of this?'

'I know it from legend – and from the holy ones.'

I noticed that his chair, gently rocking before, was now stable.

'My kin. What of them, if I go?'

'They'll go to their home as planned, with Kami, Drion and a guard of Brach warriors. All in all, it will be quite the company. I look forward to it.'

'You?'

'Yes. I will also go – to share for one last time a fireside with Annan, my old friend. We can tell each other stories as we await your return, before I too take my final journey – from this life into the next.'

This saddened me, for Annan too was old and a journey of a hundred moons or more might not give me the chance to see him again in this world. I felt a pang of loss and with it, a sense of fear, of foreboding. Aehmir must have seen this for suddenly he got to his feet, placed an arm on my shoulder and said, 'There are none fitter than such as you to take the journey to holy Kalas. The *Solon*, as you call it, will be your guide. One day, I am sure, you *will* return to the house of your mothers and fathers. You will not be the same – but then, whoever is?'

I lifted my head and looked up at him. His eyes were twinkling. I felt a weariness in my heart. Despite the reservations about leaving my friends, I had got used to the idea of going home. 'So, then, Aehmir, how am I, a mere mortal Albin Otar, already a stranger in a strange land, to attempt such a journey?'

'With me,' came a loud voice from the doorway. I turned to see Bran striding forward, his face wreathed in smiles. He slapped my back. 'Someone has to watch yer rear end, brother.'

Then Tiroc Og was there, smiling broadly. 'Yeh can't get rid of us that easily,' he said, beckoning someone else to enter: Lakon, whose awesome bravery and skills were an asset in any dangerous adventure. He came over and warmly took my hand. 'The privilege to come with yeh would be mine, brother… if yeh'd have me.' At this my eyes began to prick. It seemed that the adventure had already been planned. Once again, my fate seemed to be partially in the hands of others. I felt humbled – and suddenly less afraid.

Aehmir stood, walked over to the doorway and looked up and down the street. 'Where is she…?' he muttered, looking irritated.

She. Who? I looked at him, puzzled.

'Your company is not yet complete,' he said. Then with a shrug of his shoulders, he returned to his chair. Who did he mean?

'Our friend will be here soon, Aehmir,' said Tiroc Og assuredly. Then taking the sage to one side, they conversed with their backs to me. I looked at Bran. He and Lakon were both beaming. What on earth was going on? I must have reddened.

A gentle step then sounded from the alley, followed by a light laugh. An unmistakeable silhouette crossed the threshold into the light, long mane flaming bright in the firelight. I started to my feet, my chest fluttering wildly.

CARYN

I drew breath and folded shut the first folio of Osian's remarkable chronicle. The fire had died, though neither of us had noticed. I was just about to suggest retiring when Caryn, snapping suddenly out of her reverie, said, 'Who was it? Was it Cana-Din? Or Gimin – the Fox-Wolf? Tell me, don't leave me in suspense.'

'I can't do that, Caryn,' I laughed. 'It would break the code of all tale-tellers. You'll have to wait until I read the next part of his journal.' Of course, I'd just made that up. Were she to know, at this point in her father's adventure, without knowing everything else, I feared for what she might do. She might be of age, but as yet without enough warrior training to do anything about it – or go anywhere.

'But it's not a tale, Guardian,' she said sharply.

'It's a tale all right, Caryn. Just not a tall one.'

She just grimaced in response and raised her eyes to the roof. There was a retort coming – though I was a little taken aback by it.

''Anyway, I know you're Drion. You were there!'

'Yes, cook and flagon washer to a bunch of ungrateful renegades.' I laughed, clutching instinctively for where my arm once was and still felt it to be. Of course it was a giveaway, maybe that and my famous fishmeal porridge. In the many winters we'd been here on this island she'd only ever known me as "Guardian" and to Osian, Yamis and his sons, I was always "Uncle". To the others I was always Uscan, the Ironese for "One-Arm".

'You must really be old now!' She giggled, with maybe a guilty look.

'Careful – I'll send you out there for the wood!'

'You wouldn't. Sorry.'

She went quiet, her look puzzled, maybe trying to make all the connections. Then she asked, 'You were left back in the marshes to wait for them. So, what happened next?'

'After a few days a harrier came with a message. I was to make sure the boats were well hid, then go east through the creeks to meet with a Brach escort who would take me to Amon's house in Clachoile, to wait in that place for my friends return from Rakhaus – that is, if they returned. Had to abandon the boats, of course, but they'll still be there – should there be a next time.'

'Next time? I…'

I shook my head. She was brimming with questions; desperate to know more. But I was exhausted. That was it for the night. The rest of the story would have to wait. 'Fire's died. We have a busy day tomorrow and we'll probably have to dig our way out through thon snow if we're to go to get our supplies from Yamis – maybe stay over at the steading if there's another blizzard.'

'You mean in the top of the barn above those smelly goats,' she replied.

'But it's the warmest place there – think of those new kids you get to coddle.'

'I suppose,' she said. Usually, she liked going there. It was full of animals and small Barod grandchildren and the chores were gentle – and the best bit for her was no *Askrit* learning. 'The rest of the story?' She queried. 'When do I hear that?' But she too was yawning. She too was tired.

'I could take it with us,' I said. Then thought better of it. 'It'll keep – for when we're back here.' She nodded sleepily and again muttered, 'I suppose,' and wandered over to the wooden ladder which led up into the roof where her cosy bed chamber was. So, I folded the chronicle back into the Eronn cloth along with the second volume and put the folio away.

I sat by the fire, contemplating Osian's story, puzzling over the bits that I could never figure out. After a while, I stood up to put damp ashes over the fire so that it would stay in overnight, when there came a loud rap at the door. It was in the deep night. No-one ever called at such a time.

'Who on Yahl's earth?' I muttered, reaching for the handle of my long axe. 'Who's there, at this *hora*?' I shouted.

'Drion? Let me enter.' came a strangled response, barely audible, the voice so weak, the tribe I couldn't tell.

Cautiously I lifted the latch, leaving the chain in place and looked through the gap. Thigh deep in the drifted snow stood a familiar, hooded figure in tattered, bloodstained furs glimmering in the moonlight, long sword sheathed at the waist; backpack slung loosely over the shoulders. Only the area around the mouth was visible under the hood, scarred and streaked with faded warpaint. The shoulders were hunched; body faltering – almost ready to collapse.

'Yes, 'tis me, Drion.'

'Great Yahl,' I muttered, dropping the axe and hurriedly unbolting the door, hardly able to believe what I was seeing.

Remembering old friends:
Raj Murch, Philippa Francis, David McIntyre
and Peter Dixon